The Woman Who Lost Her Soul

Recovering the U.S. Hispanic Literary Heritage

Board of Editorial Advisors

The Woman Who Lost Her Soul

AND OTHER STORIES

Jovita González

Edited, with an Introduction, by Sergio Reyna

Recovering the U.S. Hispanic Literary Heritage

Arte Público Press
Houston, Texas

This volume is made possible through grants from the Rockefeller Foundation and the City of Houston through the Cultural Arts Council of Houston, Harris County.

Recovering the past, creating the future

Arte Público Press
University of Houston
Houston, Texas 77204-2174

Cover design by Ken Bullock

González, Jovita, 1904-1983.
[Short stories]
    The woman who lost her soul / by Jovita González; edited with an introduction by Sergio Reyna.
        p.   cm. — (Recovering the U.S. Hispanic Literary Heritage)
ISBN 1-55885-313-8 (pbk. : alk. paper)
    1. Mexican American — Fiction. 2. Texas—Social life and customs — Fiction. 3. Mexico—Social life and customs — Fiction. 4. Animals — Fiction. I. Reyna, Sergio. II. Title.
III. Series: Recovering the U.S. Hispanic Literary Heritage Project publication.
PS3563.I6947 A6 2000
813'.54—dc21   00-056605
                                                          CIP

♾ The paper used in this publication meets the requirements of the American National Standard for Information Sciences—Permanence of Paper for Printed Library Materials, ANSI Z39.48-1984.

0 1 2 3 4 5 6 7 8 9   10 9 8 7 6 5 4 3 2 1

To Dr. Nicolás Kanellos
with admiration for the invaluable guidance and
precious time he devoted to the execution of this project

And

To my dear friends Connie Evans Seaman and Alejandra
Balestra with all gratitude for their unconditional help
and academic interest in the development of this work

Contents

Acknowledgments

I thank Thomas Kreneck, head of the Special Collections and Archives, Texas A&M University—Corpus Christi Bell Library Archives, for his gracious assistance in the searching throughout the E. E. Mireles and Jovita González de Mireles Papers, for unpublished folk tales of Jovita González.

I appreciate the invaluable cooperation and academic courtesy of María Cotera, for making possible the publication in this anthology of Jovita González's priceless manuscript "Shades of the Tenth Muses." María Cotera has been working a literary project on the manuscript "Shades of the Tenth Muses" to be published in the near future.

I am also grateful, for support and help I received during the development of this project, to Alejandra Balestra, Elena Byars, Mary Calderón-Hill, Connie Evans Seaman, Claudia Garza, Pedro Garza, Sandra Montes, Greg Perrine, and Eloise Smith. I appreciate their invaluable contributions.

Publication of this compilation would not be possible without the generous support of the Recovering the U.S. Hispanic Literary Heritage Project conducted by Dr. Nicolás Kanellos.

Introduction

My sister Tula and I did everything together. We went horseback riding to the pastures with my grandfather, took long walks with father, and visited the homes of the cowboys and the ranch hands. We enjoyed the last the most. There were Tío Patricio, the mystic; Chon, who was so ugly, poor fellow, he reminded us of a toad; Old Remigio who wielded the *metate* with the dexterity of peasant women and made wonderful *tortillas.* Tía Chita whose stories about ghosts and witches made our hair stand on end, Pedro, the hunter and traveler, who had been as far as Sugar Land and had seen black people with black wool for hair, one-eyed Manuelito, the ballad singer, Tío Camilo; all furnished ranch lore in our young lives.

—Jovita González, in *Dew on the Thorn*

It is indisputable that as a whole the works of Jovita González represent a valuable artifact of the history and culture of south Texas at the beginning of the twentieth century and are an indispensable element in the recovery of the literary legacy of Mexican Americans. Jovita González is considered by some critics today as a pioneer of Mexican-American literature because she achieved success as an educator, writer, and folklorist, despite the adversities that she faced as a Hispanic woman within a society and an epoch in which intellectual matters were almost exclusively dominated by Anglo American men.

The novels, short stories, and literary essays of Jovita González are based on her experience as a native of south Texas. The many stories and legends that she preserved through her literary work were influenced by her childhood experiences and became an important part of her personal history. They also represent the history and culture of an almost forgotten minority population in the United States. Most of the stories gathered in this collection were published by González in well-known Texas magazines, such as *Southwest Review* and *Texas Folk-Lore Society Publications,* from the 1920s to the 1940s. They encompass diverse themes that can be classified as: Tales of Human Characters; Animal Tales; Religious Tales; Tales of Mexican Ancestors; Tales of Ghosts, Demons and Buried Treasures; and Tales of Popular Customs. She based her classification on the practice of the leading folklorists of her time, such as Juan B. Rael, Aurelio Espinosa, Aurora Lucero White-Lea, and J. Frank Dobie. Although this classification is not rigid, exhaustive, or definitive, it does serve us today in grouping and studying her works.

The Life of Jovita González[1]

Jovita González was born in 1904 in Roma, a small town in south Texas on the Mexican border. She was the daughter of Jacobo González Rodríguez, a descendant of a family of educators and craftsmen, and of Severina Guerra Barrera, who came from a family of colonists who participated in the settling of Nuevo Santander, a province of New Spain. Her great grandfather, who lived 125 years, received a large grant from the king of Spain and became one of the most prominent landowners in the Nuevo Santander.

At a time when higher education was often beyond the reach of minority groups, Jovita González obtained her Bachelor's degree along with a teaching certificate in History and Spanish from Our Lady of the Lake College in San Antonio, Texas. After teaching at Saint Mary's Hall in San Antonio, she went on to continue her education at the University of Texas at Austin and obtained her Master of Arts in 1930. Her Master's thesis, entitled *Social Life in Cameron, Starr, and Zapata Counties,* is a well-documented study of the culture of the inhabitants of those counties of predominant Mexican population.

During her studies at the University of Texas in 1925, Jovita González met J. Frank Dobie, a well-known pioneer in the study of folklore. With Dobie's help, González began researching Mexican folklore in Texas and became an outstanding member of the Texas Folk-Lore Society. She served both as vice-president and as president of the society whose members included teachers as well as professionals in the study of folklore. The Texas Folk-Lore Society became an important catalyst in the preservation of Texas folklore in the early twentieth century. Jovita González also served as vice-president and president of LULAC (League of United Latin American Citizens), which represented one of the first attempts by Mexican Americans to establish their own ideology in order to safeguard their rights as American citizens. González was also an active member of the Panamerican Club of Corpus Christi, which sponsored cultural and social events.

As a result of her thesis, *Social Life in Cameron, Starr, and Zapata Counties,* and through the recommendation of Dobie, González was awarded a Rockefeller Foundation Grant in 1934. This grant allowed her to take a leave of absence for a year from her teaching position at Saint Mary's Hall in San Antonio, Texas, and to dedicate herself to full-time research on the culture of south Texas. The result of this year-long research project was the writing of two novels never published in her lifetime: *Caballero: A Historical Novel,* a literary accomplishment highlighting the customs and traditions of south Texas, and *Dew on the Thorn,* a novel with a folkloric base composed of a series of short stories that were also published in various magazines and literary journals.

In 1935 Jovita González married Edmundo Mireles, who was also a teacher. In 1939 they moved from Del Rio, Texas to Corpus Christi, where they became respected educators in the Corpus Christi School District. After her marriage, González limited her folklore writing and focused most of her time and effort on teaching Spanish and on being a wife (Kreneck 77). In collaboration with her husband, Jovita produced textbooks for learning the Spanish language. She continued to teach Spanish and Texas history until her retirement from W. B. Ray High School in Corpus Christi, Texas in 1966. The Spanish textbooks she wrote were used for many years in support of bilingual education in the southwestern United States. Jovita González and her husband died in 1983 and 1987, respectively, without children or close relatives to claim the inheritance of a literary legacy that included the novels that were published posthumously and the tales in this collection.

The Folklore and the Literary Work of Jovita González

In the twentieth century two schools of thought developed regarding the scholarly treatment of folk narrative: preservation of the oral tradition in its original form, or transformation of the oral tradition by means of refinement and literary polish. Both tendencies, not surprisingly, originated a series of discussions and theoretical justifications for their methods in recovering folk narratives for preservation and analysis.

One of the folklorists who supported the first tendency was Jakob Grimm, who considered a popular story as a sacred relic of times passed, and as part of a precious treasure whose care is the responsibility of men across the ages (Cortazar 29). To maintain the original integrity of the work, a loyal reproduction does not change any of the oral text represented in oral tradition. The followers of this purist school criticized the liberty of the folk-lorists who embellished the oral tradition. This purist approach is, in fact, the one that dominates the study of folklore today. Among the folklorists in the United States who strived in the early twentieth century to maintain the oral tradition in its origi-nal form were Aurelio M. Espinosa and Juan B. Rael.[2] These folklorists preserved material from the oral tradition of the His-panics of the southwestern United States, presenting the oral tra-dition with all the slang, dialects, and the nuances of oral speech of the various social groups.

One of the followers of the opposite school of thought embraced by those who leaned toward the literary embellishment of the oral narratives was J. Frank Dobie, Jovita González's men-tor. As Limón states (*Caballero* xix), Dobie's method was edu-cated and literary but in an open-ended way. Friendship and group dynamics were evidenced in his folkloric material and were a vehicle for what J. Frank Dobie called *flavor* in the text. He attempted to enjoy the nuances of culture without analyzing or commenting on the social significance. Dobie firmly believed that folk narrative should serve as the basis for literary production, even for more elaborate narrative works, such as the novels to be written by educated literary authors. But one of the problems that is presented by this type of re-written narrative polished by the folklorist is that it is not possible to study in the text the exact nature of its effects with respect to voice, gesture, and narrative art (Thompson 449-450). To a certain extent, the text is contaminat-ed by the author's pen. The study of the art of folklore cannot be based on texts selected at random, unless they have been present-ed in their original form. Unfortunately, according to Stith Thompson, many collectors of folk narratives have been more interested in presenting stories in a manner attractive to potential purchasers than in preserving texts for scientific study (450).

As a follower of J. Frank Dobie, Jovita González became a literary elaborator of folklore. Folklorists of the stature of Aurelio M. Espinosa exercised a strong influence on Jovita González with regard to her determination in dedicating herself to the preservation of the oral tradition of her people, but it was Dobie who armed her with a methodology and a literary mind set. Jovita González collected folk narratives from her daily contact with the common people since her childhood. She collected and/or remembered a vast number of detailed stories. She polished and enhanced the original narrations that circulated among the Mexican population of south Texas, according to her "own fancy and taste," as Stith Thompson (450) characterizes this procedure when he talks about such folklorists. The work of González resulted in the production of short stories or sketches based on legends and folk tales that, because of their form and content, were pleasing to readers who preferred a refined quality of literature.

The Historic Framework of González's Literary Work

The work of Jovita González covers several important periods of colonial Texas history, including the period of Mexican domination, the period of the Texas Republic, and finally the period of U. S. statehood. González preserved important elements of the sociohistorical reality of Texas that permit the researcher to reconstruct interesting scenes of the history and folklore of the community. María Cotera, in her epilogue to the novel *Caballero,* considers that González´s work represents an early and important intent to give a place to the Chicano voice during a period in which Chicanos were witnesses to the Anglo American construction of official Texas history (339-345).

In the novels of Jovita González, especially in her novel *Dew on the Thorn,* we can clearly appreciate the historic framework for her literary creativity. *Dew on the Thorn* documents details in the lives of González's Hispanic-Mestizo ancestors who lived in the 1740s in what is now Texas. This was during the last large scale exploration by the Spaniards in the New World. The novel makes reference to the relative autonomy and tranquillity of life after the Spanish government was expelled as a result of the Mexican War of Independence of 1810 and prior to U.S. statehood. As the community developed, its first real crisis was, for González, the invasion by the United States.

In the novel *Caballero,* González details the political and social character of the times, placing life in south Texas within the context of change brought about by U.S. expansionism and its appropriation of Mexico's northern states. Limón points out that Texas aided the expansion of the United States by declaring itself an independent republic in 1836 after the defeat of Santa Anna at San Jacinto, an event documented in *Caballero* along with the recounting of the fall of the Alamo (*Caballero* xii-xii). Mexico refused to recognize the loss of Texas in 1836, especially the territory located between the Rio Grande and the Rio Nueces, now south Texas. The conflicts between Mexico and the United States culminated in war from 1846 to 1848. The signing of the Treaty of Guadalupe Hidalgo obliged Mexico to surrender its territories, including the disputed parts of Texas, to the United States. Both culturally and from a perspective of power, the direct and immediate opposition to the Americans is fully and explicitly highlighted in *Caballero.*

In *Caballero,* a panorama is presented of the historic reality in which the protagonist lived in the 1840s. Limón detailed this panorama as a climate of political discontent, of discrimination, and of hostilities toward the Mexican American population (xii-xiv). *Caballero* was not published at the time that it was created because it was not accepted by the publishing houses, despite González's having recruited an Anglo American co-author to make it more palatable to prospective publishers. The manuscript was later reported lost by E. E. Mireles and Jovita González, during an interview with Marta Cotera in the 1970s, because the Mireleses feared political repercussions which could threaten their teaching careers in Corpus Christi, Texas (*Caballero* xviii-xxii). In the 1970s the political climate was still volatile, reminiscent of the racial climate of the 1930s and 1940s in south Texas. The Mireleses refused to publish the manuscripts even when the Chicano Movement was at its height. The manuscripts were finally published two decades later through the efforts of researchers José E. Limón and María Cotera .

The other narratives and the academic essays published by Jovita González described the climate of discrimination experienced by Mexican Americans in Texas. This discrimination occurred within the cultural context characterized by customs and traditions that place man at the center of the world and woman as subservient and submissive to men, as well as in the national context of racial discrimination against Mexican Americans, who were forced to be subservient to Anglo Saxons.

Although Jovita González pointed out these differences and problems between Anglos and Mexicans, it is possible to say that her intent was not to emphasize the differences between them, but to preserve the customs and traditions that identified her people by honoring them through writing, for they would perish in oral form, given the transformations of social life occurring rapidly in the Southwest as Anglo dominance increased. But, above all, González wished to create threads of understanding between these two ideologically and culturally opposed groups that found themselves in the historic necessity of sharing the same geography.

It was extremely difficult for a woman to study, write, and publish literary works at this time. Jovita González's accomplishments and literary successes are even more admirable for a Hispanic woman because of the degree of patriarchy in the society in which she was raised. Tatum marvels that at a time when the Mexican Americans had limited opportunities to become educated, González obtained her teaching certificate (225). Limón was surprised by the daring attitude of a young woman exposing her work in a society where writing and lecturing were almost exclusively done by men: "What is she thinking, this young Texas-Mexican woman in a roomful of largely male Anglos in 1930?" (*Dancing* 68).

In summary, it can be affirmed that the historic framework adopted by González for her literary works is characterized by the political and social conflicts between the conquered and the conquerors. At the root of this daily battle played out in Texas was the social climate, which was permeated with violence and the violation of the most basic norms of social convention. Both groups exhibited attitudes of racial and cultural prejudice toward everything foreign. At the internal level, within the Hispanic culture of the southwestern United States, González knowingly depicted in her novels, essays, folk tales, and legends, the patriarchal system in which women were seen as having an insignificant role in the political and social development of the community. The situation of racial conflict, discrimination, and the undervaluing of women, which prevailed in the period described in her writings (middle of the nineteenth century), continued to exist, although to a lesser extent, during the years when Jovita González published the majority of her works: the 1930s and 1940s.

The Literary Works of Jovita González

The literary works of Jovita González have as their primary objective the historic preservation through the written word of the oral tradition in particular and Hispanic culture in general.

The object of study that is evident in each one of her works—whether they are novels, stories, legends or essays—is the description of the folklore of the Hispanic community. Among others, the themes that are addressed in her literary works include the cowboy, the peon, the patriarchal system of the family, and the static role of men and women within the hierarchy of Tejano culture.

The works of Jovita González represent a *native literature,* which reflects the economic, social, and political implications resulting from minority group membership in the United States. Her works are imprinted with the sense of history and tradition of the Hispanic population that has lived for many years in south Texas. As Velázquez-Treviño affirms, Jovita González exhibits a strong social conscience that takes into account the socioeconomic problems of her ethnic group (Jovita González 76-83). Through her folkloric narratives, González protests against the discrimination practiced by the Anglo-Saxon community against Mexicans during the colonization of Texas. In addition, Velázquez-Treviño emphasizes that the prose of Jovita González reveals the desire to reaffirm and vindicate the vision of her social group that was repressed and discriminated against during the colonization of the Southwest (83). It should be clarified that González, in her literary works, denounced the abuses and injustices of Anglo Americans towards Mexicans in Texas and also maintained the hope of influencing the culture of the United States through exposure to her literature. She wanted to create bridges of tolerance and mutual understanding between the two groups that would permit cohabitation founded on mutual respect.

Chase (123) and Garza-Falcón (74-75) maintain that Jovita González produced her essays and her picturesque folkloric narrations from the perspective of the upper class. Although González's ancestors were privileged in early nineteenth-century Tejano society, her own family was lower middle class. She had to work to support her family and to finance her studies at the university because her family could not afford to pay her expenses (*Dew on the Thorn* xxiii). The fact that González was able to write about popular culture of the Hispanic community can be explained by her more humble social standing and her association with the working classes. And this led her to identify with the cowboy, the peon, the vagabond, and in general with the disinherited Mexican community in south Texas.

As a writer, Jovita González was a nativist, precisely because her work documents the priority of Mexican American culture in south Texas and its enduring legacy. It is precisely the written preservation of Mexican American oral lore that represented for her the protection and maintenance of her culture in the face of obliteration by the growing Anglo presence in Texas. It is by means of the enduring presence of art as an element in the continuity of the culture and sequential time that the work of Jovita González captures life's ephemeral images and rescues them from the imminent danger of obscurity, thereby making them available for our contemplation (Bruce-Novoa 95-96). According to Bruce-Novoa, in these images we encounter a permanent reflection of the essence of our being. This sacred act gives meaning to individual actions and thereby gives meaning to our world. Therefore, fortified with the recognition of our true significance and purpose, we can resist or face the chaos that threatens our existence. Literature becomes not just a propitious space from which to respond to chaos; even more importantly, it becomes an answer in itself (96-99). Thus, we can affirm that the literary works of Jovita González are an enduring response in the face of the imminent dissipation of the values, roots and cultural traditions of Mexican Americans.

While respected and admired during her career as a high school teacher and lecturer on Hispanic history and culture, Jovita González was particularly appreciated by a later generation of Chicano scholars for her pioneering literary efforts (Kreneck 77). Jovita González is considered by some academics, such as José Limón, Gloria Louise Vázquez-Treviño, Charles Tatum, Teresa Palomo Acosta, and Diana Rebolledo, among others, as one of the first Mexican American writers and folklorists. At a time when it was rare for Mexican Americans to distinguish themselves in academia, González had won a place for herself among Texas intellectuals. González was also one of the first to identify and write about her people as natives of the Southwest. Her essays and research, thus, have great potential for the reconstruction of Mexican American cultural history.

As a literary stylist, González has caught the attention of a number of critics who have been reconstructing Mexican American literary history. The charm of her tales has captivated them for various obvious reasons. González's folkloric narratives are humorous, vivid, and colorful. They usually begin with a description of the character who will become the protagonist of the story (Chase 123), and the resulting anecdotes are always curious and intriguing. González's subtle humor and art of description bring these characters to life (Tatum 234). Her critical stance is represented in such narratives through irony and caricature, although this somewhat distances her from her creatures (*Cultural Ambivalence* 95).

González's folkloric tales are like snapshots of people that reveal their innermost thoughts and motivation. According to Tatum, González captured in her writing the essence of the people and scenery that were an important part of her childhood (226). She was particularly drawn to the world of the cowboy and portrays him as a special personage, born in Texas as the product of an interracial mix of the Amerindian and the Spanish conqueror (Chase 123). From his indigenous ancestors the cowboy inherited his love of nature and freedom, as well as his melancholy and fatalism. From his Spanish ancestors he inherited his love of music, his poetry, and religious devotion. Within his conception of life, the cowboy maintained a series of myths that found meaning in nature. Such myths and legends as "El Cenizo," "The Mocking Bird," "El Cardo Santo," "The Guadalupana Vine," "The Cicada," "The Cardinal," "The Woodpecker," "The Paisano," "The Dove,"

"Legends of Ghosts and Treasures," "The Devil on the Border," and "Without a Soul," among many others, preserved and transmitted his values from one generation to the next.

It is important to point out that some of the narratives that Jovita González published in *Southwest Review, LULAC News,* and *Texas Folk-Lore Society Publications* were later incorporated in her novel *Dew on the Thorn:* "Tío Patricio," "The First Cactus Blossom," "The Gift of the Pitahaya," "Legends of Ghosts and Treasures," "Without a Soul," and "The Mocking Bird." According to the novel's editor, José E. Limón, *Dew on the Thorn* can be interpreted as a unified literary combination of brief narratives that are inserted into the short novel, where the life of the community of Mexican descendants in south Texas is revealed (xv). Garza-Falcón asserts that most of the author's presentations at the annual meetings of the Texas Folklore Society and her contributions to their publications were actually derived from this earlier manuscript of *Dew on the Thorn* (81-82). In this novel, a somewhat disguised plot line links a group of short folktales. These stories, told by various characters in the novel, are digressions that expand the narrative. González later used these stories as material for her various folklore presentations and publications.

One of the key individuals promoting the oral tradition of the Mexican American community is without doubt the *storyteller.* González describes the *storyteller* within his or her natural setting as the central figure surrounded by an audience that has gathered precisely to enjoy the stories. Thus, narratives such as "Tío Patricio," "The Bullet-Swallower," "Ambrosio the Indian," "Pedro the Hunter," and "The Mail Carrier," in and of themselves, celebrate and preserve the *storyteller* as an historian and transmitter of values for the community. In "Shelling the Corn by Moonlight," for example, González commemorates the typical custom of the early Hispanic settlers of meeting together at night by the light of the campfire and the moon to tell ghost stories and tales of buried treasure:

> It was on a night like this that the ranch folk gathered at the Big House to shell corn. All came: Tío Julianito, the pastor, with his brood of black half-starved children ever eager for food; Alejo the fiddler; Juanito the idiot, called the Innocent, because the Lord was keeping his mind in Heaven; Pedro the hunter, who had seen the world and spoke English; the *vaqueros;* and, on rare occasions, Tío Esteban, the mail carrier. Even the women came, for on such occasions supper was served.
>
> A big canvas was spread outside, in front of the kitchen. In the center of this canvas ears of corn were piled in pyramids for the shellers, who sat about in a circle and with their bare hands shelled the grains off the cobs.
>
> It was then, under the moonlit sky, that we heard stories of witches, buried treasures, and ghosts. (*Among My People* 100)

In addition to emphasizing the personality of the cowboy, the peon, and the preacher, Jovita González points out the strong presence of the landowner within the patriarchal system full of myths and superstitions; he, in particular, is threatened by the new political and social order imposed by the Anglo Americans. In "Don Tomás" and "Don José María," the author tells of two rich landowners who, typically, control not only their own families but also the lives of their peons and other employees. The power that these landowners maintain over the population of the region is not only seen as exercised directly over their workers and families, but also in the creation and imposition of their laws and their fight against the imminent overthrow of the patriarchal system.

In her tales of the animal kingdom, such as "The Paisano," "The Mocking Bird," "The Cicada," and "The Woodpecker," González illustrates the values worthy of transmission from one generation to the next: honesty, humility, and fidelity, among others. Velázquez-Treviño has written an interesting analysis of how González's stories detail the lives of wild animals, mirroring in the animal kingdom the limited women in a patriarchy, where the men are the center of daily life (*Cultural Ambivalence* 101-102). They receive the attention of all who surround them, while women are submissive and must sacrifice their well-being for the men around whom their world revolves.

González's preservation of the folklore of her people would not be complete without the preservation of the supernatural, a theme that is vital in Mexican American oral tradition. Legends about ghosts, demons, and buried treasure that were passed down from the Spaniards, are represented in "The Devil on the Border," "Legends of Ghosts and Treasures," "Nana Chita," and "Without a Soul."

Jovita González also sought to preserve the memory of her Mexican ancestors. In "The Gift of the Pitahaya," she presents a "prince from the faraway land of the Aztecs (75). He was tall and straight and walked the village streets in pride and disdain. His look was bold and defiant like the eagle's. The feather mantle he wore rivaled in beauty the flowers of the prairie. Heavy bracelets of gold and precious stones circled his arms." Through this story, González demonstrates the pride, veneration, and nostalgia for the indigenous roots of Mexican culture. "Ambrosio the Indian" and "The First Cactus Blossom" are stories that also deal with characters and themes related to Amerindian ancestry. In these stories, González shares with her readers an overflowing pride for her Aztec race, the bronze race, the race of true heroes that have contributed to the country of "her people," such important figures as Moctezuma, Cuauhtémoc, Benito Juárez, The Pípila, José María Morelos, and others.

"Shades of the Tenth Muses"[3] was never published by Jovita González. In this story, González exhibits great pride in her Mexican ancestry. Evidently, this is the only non-folkloric story she wrote. Here, she describes the natural beauty and splendor of Mexico, and gives evidence of her Amerindian ancestry when she writes that "a Virgin of Guadalupe reminds [her] daily that [she is] a descendant of a proud stoic race" (80). González describes Mexican social classes of the seventeenth century and expresses her enormous admiration for the Mexican nun, Sor Juana Inés de la Cruz, because of the intense intellectual virtues that made her stand out as one of the most important female writers of seventeenth century in the Spanish speaking world. While demonstrating clear admiration for the *Tenth Muse,* Sor Juana Inés de la Cruz, Jovita González also deals with the role of women and the defense of their rights in the patriarchial society of seventeenth-century Mexico.

The political resistance of the Mexican American to oppression is one of the last themes that González developed toward the end of her writing career. In the penultimate story that she published, "The Bullet-Swallower," she writes of a smuggler who defies the laws imposed by the Anglos and enforced by the Texas Rangers. This rogue-hero, related to the heroes of border ballads, survives an armed confrontation with the Texas Rangers after being shot in the mouth and scarred for life, to which he owes his nickname *Bullet-Swallower.* Limón suggests that in "The Bullet Swallower" Jovita González reveals "more of her narratively unrepressed critical political unconscious" (*Dancing* 71-74). Her criticism of the North American invasion of Texas and of the subsequent imposition of rules and laws on the Hispanic community is manifested in such attitudes of obvious resistance on the part of the Mexican American community. These attitudes of resistance were evidenced by the Mexicans through the defiance of the laws imposed by the new government, specifically those regarding smuggling and gambling. This attitude of explicit resistance, in an attempt to wage a fierce although disadvantaged fight against the Texas Rangers, is illustrated in the following passage from "The Bullet Swallower":

> The men I associated with were neither sissies nor saints. . . . We were bringing several cartloads of smuggled goods to be delivered at once and in safety to the owner. Oh, no, the freight was not ours but we would have fought for it with our life's blood. . . . The pack mules, loaded with packages wrapped in tanned hides, we led by the bridle. We hid the mules in a clump of tules and were just beginning to dress when the Rangers fell upon us. Of course we did not have a stitch of clothes on; did you think we swam fully dressed? Had we but had our guns in readiness, there might have been a different story to tell. We would have fought like wild-cats to keep the smuggled goods from falling into their hands. It was not ethical among smugglers to lose the property of a Mexican to Americans, and as to falling ourselves into their hands, we preferred death a thousand of times. It's not disgrace and dishonor to die like a man, but it is to die like a rat. . . . I ran to where the pack mules were to get my gun. Like a fool that I was I kept yelling at the top of my voice, 'You so, so, and so gringo cowards, why don't you attack men like men? Why do you wait until they are undressed and unarmed?' I must have said some very insulting things, for one of them shot at me right in the mouth. The bullet knocked all of my front teeth out, grazed my tongue and went right through the back of my neck. Didn't kill me,

though. It takes more than bullets to kill Antonio Traga-
Balas . . . (108-09)

Thus, toward the end of her creative writing career, Jovita
González achieves the explicit expression of this typically Mexican American attitude of resistance. In the "Bullet-Swallower,"
Jovita González ultimately achieves the vision, clarity, and political as well as social focus that are defined and refined throughout her work and that came to dominate Chicano writing in the
1960s and 1970s.

As Tey Diana Rebolledo points out in her studies of Chicano
literary tradition, as more and more texts are saved from
anonymity, we gain a better understanding of the impact of
women on the political and social structure of the country
throughout history (26-27). González is certainly one of our fore-
bears whose literary works should be studied in depth.

Sergio Reyna
University of Houston

Notes

[1]More information about the biography of Jovita González can be found in *E. E. Mireles and Jovita González de Mireles Papers, Special Collection & Archives, Texas A&M University-Corpus Christi Bell Library*. Also, more biographical information can be found in Jovita González, *Dew on the Thorn*, ed. José E. Limón (Houston: Arte Público,1997): ix-xiii.

[2]See Aurelio M. Espinosa, *Cuentos populares españoles* (New York: AMS, 1967) and Juan B. Rael, *Cuentos españoles de Colorado y Nuevo Méjico* (New York: Arno, 1977).

[3]This story was recently located by María Cotera in the enormous collection of manuscripts catalogued with the title *E. E. Mireles and Jovita González de Mireles Papers, Special Collection & Archives, Texas A&M University-Corpus Christi Bell Library*. At the time of the publication of this anthology of short stories written by Jovita González, "Shades of the Tenth Muses" still had not been published. At this writing, María Cotera has been working on this story and is about to publish a literary analysis.

Works Cited

Bruce-Novoa, Juan. "The Space of Chicano Literature Update: 1978." *Retrospace: Collected Essays on Chicano Literature.* Houston: Arte Público, 1990.

Chase, Cida S. "Jovita González de Mireles (1899-1983)." *Dictionary of Literary Biography.* Ed. Francisco Lomelí. Detroit: Gale Research, 1992.

Cortazar, Augusto Raúl. *Bosquejo de una introducción al folklore.* Tucumán, Arg.: Universidad de Tucumán—Departamento de Investigaciones Regionales—Instituto de Historia, Lingüística y Folklore, 1941.

Cotera, María. Epilogue. *Caballero: A Historical Novel.* By Jovita González and Eve Raleigh. Ed. José E. Limón and María Cotera. College Station: Texas A&M University, 1996.

Garza-Falcón, Leticia M. *Gente decente. A Borderlands Response to the Rhetoric of Dominance.* Austin: University of Texas, 1998.

González, Jovita. "The Gift of the Pitahaya." *Man, Bird, and Beast.* Ed. J. Frank Dobie. Austin: Texas Folk-Lore Society, 1930.

———. "Among My People." *Tone the Bell Easy.* Ed. J. Frank Dobie. Austin: Texas Folk-Lore Society, 1932.

———. "The Bullet-Swallower." *Puro Mexicano.* Ed. J. Frank Dobie. Austin: Texas Folk-Lore Society, 1935.

———. *Dew on the Thorn.* Ed. José E. Limón. Houston: Arte Público, 1997.

———. *Shades of the Tenth Muses*. Ms. Special Collection & Archives, Texas A&M University-Corpus Christi Bell Library.

González, Jovita, and Eve Raleigh. *Caballero: A Historical Novel*. Ed. José E. Limón and María Cotera. College Station: Texas A&M University, 1996.

Kreneck, Thomas H. "Recovering the 'Lost' Manuscripts of Jovita González. The Production of South Texas Mexican-American Literature." *Texas Library Journal* Summer (1998): 76-79.

Limón, José E. Introduction. *Dew on the Thorn*. By Jovita González. Ed. José E. Limón. Houston: Arte Público, 1997.

———. Introduction. *Caballero: A Historical Novel*. By Jovita González and Eve Raleigh. Ed. José E. Limón and María Cotera. College Station: Texas A&M University, 1996.

———. *Dancing with the Devil: Society and Culture Poetics in Mexican-American South Texas*. Madison: The University of Wisconsin, 1994.

Rebolledo, Tey Diana. *Women Singing in the Snow: A Critical Analysis of Chicano Literature*. Tucson: University of Arizona, 1995.

Tatum, Charles, ed. *Mexican-American Literature*. New York: Harcourt Brace Jovanovich, 1989.

Thompson, Stith. *The Folktale*. New York: Dryden Press, 1946.

Velázquez-Treviño, Gloria Louise. "Cultural Ambivalence in Early Chicana Prose Fiction." Diss. Stanford University, 1985.

———. "Jovita González: una voz de resistencia cultural en la temprana narrativa chicana." *Mujer y literatura mexicana y chicana: culturas en contacto: primer coloquio fronterizo 22, 23 y 24 de abril de 1987*. Tijuana, Méx.: El Colegio de la Frontera Norte, 1988.

The Woman Who
Lost Her Soul

Animal Tales

The Mocking Bird

There was a time when all the creatures of Nature talked a common language. This language was Spanish. *El zenzontle,* the mocking bird, had the sweetest voice of all. The other birds stopped their flight to listen to him; the Indian lover ceased his words of love; even the talkative *arroyo* hushed. He foretold the spring, and when the days grew short and his song was no longer heard, the north winds came. Although he was not a foolish bird, *el zenzontle* was getting conceited.

"I am great, indeed," he said to his mate. "All Nature obeys me. When I sing, the blossoms hid in the trees come forth; the prairie flowers put on their gayest garments at my call and the birds begin to mate; even man, the all wise, heeds my voice and dances with joy, for the happy season draws near."

"Hush, you are foolish and conceited like all men," replied his wife. "They listen and wait for the voice of God, and when He calls, even you sing."

He did not answer his wife, for you must remember he was not so foolish after all, but in his heart he knew that he was right.

That night after kissing his wife goodnight, he said to her. "Tomorrow I will give a concert to the flowers, and you shall see them sway and dance when they hear me."

"*Con el favor de Dios,*" she replied. ("If God wills it.")

Jovita González, "Folk-Lore of the Texan-Mexican Vaquero," *Texas and Southwestern Lore,* ed. J. Frank Dobie (Austin: Folk-Lore Society, 1927) 10-11. This story was republished in "Stories of My People," *Texas Folk and Folklore,* eds. Mody C. Boatright, William H. Hudson and Allen Maxwell (Dallas: Southern Methodist U P, 1954) 20-22.

"Whether God wills it or not I shall sing," he replied angrily. "Have I not told you that the flowers obey me and not God?"

Early next morning *el zenzontle* could be seen perched on the highest limb of a huisache. He cleared his throat, coughed, and opened his bill to sing, but no sound came. For down with the force of a cyclone swooped a hawk and grabbed with his steel-like claws the slender body of the singer.

"*Con el favor de Dios, con el favor de Dios,*" he cried in distress, while he thought of his wise little wife. As he was being carried up in the air, he realized his foolishness and repented of it, and said, "O God, it is you who make the flowers bloom and the birds sing, not I." As he thought thus, he felt himself slipping and falling, falling, falling. He fell on a ploughed field, and what a fall it was. A white dove who had her nest nearby picked him up and comforted him.

"My wings," he mourned, looking at them, "how tattered and torn they look! Whatever shall I tell my wife?"

The dove took pity on him, and plucking three of her white feathers, mended his wings.

As a reminder of his foolish pride, the mockingbird to this day has the white feathers of the dove. And it is said by those who know that he never begins to sing without saying, "*con el favor de Dios.*"

The Woodpecker

Pájaro, pájaro carpintero,   Woodpecker, woodpecker,
Pájaro trabajador   You hard working bird,
Yo no te pido dinero   I am not asking for money;
Sólo te pido perdón   I merely beg your forgiveness.

Such is the rhyme which all Mexican ranch children repeat whenever they see a woodpecker. And if you ask them the meaning of it, this is the story you will hear.

In a very poor house, so poor that it had no roof, lived a man named Juan with his family. He earned his living making wooden spoons out of the slender Texas ebony tree. But as he did not like to work; and as the process of making spoons was long and tedious, his children often went hungry. One day when his wife had scolded more than usual he took his ax with a moan and a groan and went to the nearby *potrero* (pasture). Very soon he came across what he had been looking for, a straight smooth ebony. Cursing the fate that had not been content with making him a poor man but had made him lazy also, he swung his ax and began to cut. A woodpecker came out of his hole and what was Juan's surprise when the bird spoke:

"Dear friend, do not cut down my house. My little ones can not fly yet."

Jovita González, "Tales and Songs of the Texas-Mexicans," *Man, Bird and Beast,* ed. J. Frank Dobie (Austin: Folk-Lore Society, 1932) 93-95.

"I am sorry, *Carpintero,* but mine are starving and unless I make spoons out of this very tree they will die from hunger."

"Please, sir, if you leave my home you will never have to work again."

At this Juan's face brightened like the April sun after a shower.

"Really, *Carpintero?*"

"Really, my friend." And going into his hole, *Señor Carpintero* came back holding a little purse in his beak.

"Here," the bird said, "this is a magic purse. and if you ever need money hold it in your hand and say: 'Do your duty, little purse.'"

Juan was very doubtful as to the merit of the woodpecker's gift; so on his way home, just to make sure, he took it out and said the magic words. Immediately it filled with gold coins. He sang and danced with joy. Never in his life, not even in the days of his courtship, had he moved with such quickness.

That same day he went to the city. Fearing to lose his magic purse, he gave it to the landlady at an inn to keep for him.

"My dear lady, be very careful with it. You see how dirty it looks, don't you? Don't be deceived by looks, *Señora.* It is the most wonderful purse you ever saw. I leave it in your care, but whatever you do, you must not say to it: 'Do your duty, little purse.'"

It is needless to say that as soon as he was gone the woman did what she was told not to do.

Naturally, when Juan came back both the woman and the purse were gone.

So to Juan's misfortune he had to take his ax the next day and go to the pasture in search of an ebony tree. Hoping that his friend the woodpecker would come out, he started cutting on the tree.

"What?" said the woodpecker. "You here again? What did you do with the purse I gave you?"

And Juan had to tell his story. When he had finished, the woodpecker said:

"Your head is as hard as the bark of the ebony tree you are cutting. No one but you would have done that. I shall teach you a lesson that you will never forget. Here, take this whip and when you get home say, 'Whip do your duty.'"

Of course, Juan expected something wonderful, but when he uttered the words his gift was transformed into an *alicantre* (whip snake) and oh, how well it did its duty. It beat Juan out of the house, then into the house, and out again, and the faster he ran the faster the snake whipped. He climbed a mesquite tree and the snake followed.

"Only when you ask the woodpecker's pardon will I cease to whip you," said the snake.

And down to the pasture ran the poor man, the snake close at his heels. Finally they came to the ebony tree, where, falling on his knees, Juan gasped the words:

Pájaro, pájaro carpintero	Woodpecker, woodpecker,
Pájaro trabajador	You hard working bird,
Yo no te pido dinero	I do not ask you for money.
Lo que te pido es perdón	I merely ask your forgiveness.

"Very well," said the woodpecker, who had come to see what the excitement was all about. "But I am not satisfied with that. You and your children's children must ask pardon of my descendants of the trouble you have caused us."

So to this day Juan's descendants have always repeated the rhyme whenever they see a woodpecker.

The Paisano

Everyone knows that when the world was young all the creatures of nature spoke a common language and understood each other. Social classes and distinctions also prevailed among them. The eagle was the proud king of the air and all flying things, and the mocking bird had the vain glory of being the lord of the singers. In this manner all the different families with a King at their head formed a world of their own; and quarrels, jealousies and disputes were never lacking among the feathered people.

There was a bird, who, although of plebeian origin, was a distant relation of the pheasants. This made him vain, arrogant and haughty. Every evening he went walking, his crest waving in the air and his tail switching from left to right with the pride of the peacock. He did not deign to speak to the humble sparrows and the modest dove who always mourned her misfortunes. But he was only too glad to greet the nobles and the lords of high position whenever the occasion presented itself. Forgetting his humble birth, he addressed them as cousins and *paisanos*.

"Good morning, *Paisano Zenzontle,*[†] how is your Lordship?" Or "how are you, *Paisano?*" addressing the noble Sir Cardinal.

Jovita González, "Tales and Songs of the Texas-Mexicans," *Man, Bird and Beast,* ed. J. Frank Dobie (Austin: Folk-Lore Society, 1932) 92-93. This story was republished in "Stories of My People," *Texas Folk and Folklore,* eds. Mody C. Boatright, William H. Hudson and Allen Maxwell (Dallas: Southern Methodist U P, 1954) 19-20.
[†]Mocking bird.

7

His lack of common sense and his excessive vanity blinded him in such a way that he never did notice the disdain and coldness with which he was tolerated. One day while the eagle was discussing important matters of state with the nobles of the kingdom—the cardinals, the scissortails and the hawks—the foolish cousin of the pheasant family came into the chamber without announcing himself. He did not see the consternation on the face of the nobles, who were shocked at his daring, but, bowing and smiling, said to the monarch:

"How fares your Majesty and my *paisanos,* the nobles here assembled?"

The eagle, furious at seeing the familiarity with which a plebeian treated him, cried out in a voice like the tempest of a July night:

"Out of my presence, creature of low birth! I banish you forever from my kingdom. From now on you forfeit the noble name of *Faisán.* You will forget to fly and will feed on the most unclean things of the earth, snakes, tarantulas and poisonous insects."

The poor bird, blinded with shame and mortification, tried to fly from the court room but could not; his wings had lost their strength. To his greater dishonor, he was forced to run out of the room like a common beast. Since that time he has been the outcast—a pariah—of the birds. He runs here and there among the chaparral and cactus in his endeavor to hide his shame and disgrace. When the heat of the desert plains is unbearable, something like a sob is heard. It is his voice harsh and melancholy mourning the loss of his caste.

Not only the birds mock him, but man, to remind him of his pride and vanity, calls him *paisano.*

The Cicada

La *Cigarra*† was a gay person, in fact too gay to suit his wife. In spring when the *huisache* was in bloom he became intoxicated with the balmy perfumed air and the joy of living. It was then that, forgetting his duties of a faithful husband, he made love to the butterflies, which, like flying flowers, tempted him with their beauty, and to the hummingbirds, the tenors of the fields.

His wife was jealous and when her erring husband returned home in the evening, satisfied with himself and life, you should have heard her garrulous voice rise above the stillness of night. But he said nothing and merely sat heavy eyed with love and too happy to hear. As summer came on and the July heat made his life unbearable, his romantic adventurous habits were transformed into a languorous lassitude. Perched on the bark of a mesquite, he complained in his shrill voice of the cruelty of the sun. It was then that his wife, forgiving his past offenses, bathed his feverish forehead with the morning dew. The butterflies seeing him so domesticated flew to more venturesome lovers and the hummingbirds forgot him in disgust.

Jovita González, "Tales and Songs of the Texas-Mexicans," *Man, Bird and Beast,* ed. J. Frank Dobie (Austin: Folk-Lore Society, 1932) 95-96. This story was republished in "Stories of My People," *Texas Folk and Folklore,* eds. Mody C. Boatright, William H. Hudson and Allen Maxwell (Dallas: Southern Methodist U P, 1954) 22-23.
†The locust, or cicada.

All was peaceful again until spring, when passions were stirred in his heart, and his roving disposition returned. At last his wife went to the eagle, the monarch of all flying beings, and presented her plea. After due deliberation the king replied:

"Only one thing can check his roaming ways and that is to make him ugly in the sight of the ladies. From now on his eyes will be popped and round, and his colored wings an ashy gray. If this does not stop him nothing else will."

And it did, for the butterflies laughed at his owl-like eyes and colorless wings. Chagrined and morose, he came home and for months refused to speak. His wife's wishes had gone beyond her expectations; she wanted him at home, it is true, but expected him to keep her company as in the days of their courtship. Realizing that she could never be happy with this ugly creature who did nothing but complain, she went to the king again and this time asked him to make her like her husband. And with her change she became fretful like him. So to this day the shrill voices of the cicadas are heard in the heat of summer, the male complaining and shrill, the female shrill but contented.

The Cardinal

Every one regards the cardinal for the brilliancy of his feathers and the sweetness of his voice. But once he was an insignificant, ashy gray, little person noticed by none until he met and spoke with the spirit of the plains. And this is the story, a Texas tale one—of those fantastic creations of the fertile *mestizo* mind.

The singing birds were to have a concert in celebration of the arrival of spring. The mocking birds, the thrushes, the doves, and even the magpies filled the air with their songs. With the blooming of the trees and flowers and the arrival of the butterflies, enthusiasm ran riot among the feathered creatures. Crazed with joy, they sang unceasingly. All were joyous except a little gray bird who, too sensitive at his inability to sing, stayed at home. He tried to sing but just a gruff, hoarse sound came from his throat. He tried again and again but with no success. And if birds can weep, he wept in despair.

"If I could sing just for once," said the little bird, "how happy I could be."

"Why do you want to sing?" asked a voice.

"Why? Why? So I can sing a love song to my mate like all other birds do, and praise the beauty of the world."

Jovita González, "Tales and Songs of the Texas-Mexicans," *Man, Bird and Beast,* ed. J. Frank Dobie (Austin: Folk-Lore Society, 1932) 96-98.

"A wonderful thought indeed! I might help you, little bird, if I could but see your mate."

So the lady bird came.

"You are not very pretty, my dear," said the voice. "And you can not sing either?"

The little lady bird shook her head sorrowfully.

"Would you really want your husband to sing?"

"Oh, yes, yes," said the little gray wife, clasping her little claws pathetically. "We could be so happy."

"I can give beauty and voice to only one of you. Which shall it be, you or your husband?"

"My husband, if you please," said the little lady.

"Are you sure you will not regret it?" continued the voice.

"Yes, yes. You see he has to go out into the world, while I stay at home and care for my babies."

"And you," said the voice, speaking to the male, "accept the sacrifice of your wife?"

"She has chosen well," replied he in a pompous voice.

"Very well, tomorrow at dawn things will be as you wish."

And when the sun tinted the horizon with red both birds jumped from their bed in the tree top. The male was a brilliant red. They looked at each other, the female with a smile admiring the glory of her mate, the male with a frown noticing for the first time the ugliness of his wife. Then, raising his crested head, he sang. The voice was clear and triumphant, an epic in song. He soon forgot his wife's sacrifice, grew overbearing and cruel, and scolded and pecked her because of her ugliness.

But the spirit of the Plains saw all and grew sorry for the little lady bird. He could not take away the gift he had so freely given to the male, and since he could give her just one gift he made her a wonderful singer. Whereas he husband's song was one of triumph, hers became one of love and gratitude. Probably because of her unselfishness, the grayness of her dress has changed to a rosy tint. So now, whenever the male begins to fuss and scold, she, knowing the vanity of his sex, tosses her little head and flies off laughing at the stupidity of husbands, who, like hers, are all woman made and yet are proud of what they think is their own achievement.

The Mescal-Drinking Horse

The thick brush country of the Rio Grande saw his birth. His mother, a scrub mare, famous for her ability to smell and dodge the law, had saved Juan José, her smuggler master, from a prison fate. *El Viento,* she had been called, for she raced with the fleetness of the Gulf winds as they blow over the prairie, defying the thick mesquite thorns, and the screwlike spikes of the *granjeno* and the flexible but tough cactus needles. His father was a powerful stallion of Arabian blood that had wandered away from the stables of his rich master.

And so it was that *El Conejo* came into existence. An awkward creature since birth, he had been a contradiction of everything a horse should be. "He looks like a rabbit," his master had said, laughing uproariously, seeing the trembling creature with his mother's short, stubby hind legs and the powerful front legs of his Arabian father. So he was called *El Conejo* (the rabbit). He grew, a gentle, good-natured pony. Juan José's children made him their pet, spoiled him, and he in turn bore them from their home hidden in the thick chaparral to the *camino real,* where he and the children peeped with curiosity at the outside world.

One never-to-be-forgotten day, his placid life of easy-going contentment came to an abrupt end. Juan José, doubly drunk—

Jovita González, "The Mescal-Drinking Horse," *Mustang and Cow Horses,* ed. J. Frank Dobie, Mody C. Boatright, and Harry H. Ransom (Dallas: Southern Methodist U P, 1965) 396-402.

drunk both with success of his latest exploit and with a quart of *Pájaro Azul mescal*—opened a new and vicious world to him.

"Come here, Conejo," Juan José called to him, waving a newly opened bottle of *mescal.* "I don't like your looks," he laughed. "A horse like a rabbit is neither a horse nor a rabbit. I know you don't like your appearance, either. Come here to me; this will make you forget." And, saying this, he poured the quart of *mescal* into a tin wash basin.

Conejo approached the basin, and without even the faintest sniff, took a deep draught. He looked up, surprised at the fire that burned him, gave a snort and a kick, circled the pan gingerly, sniffed at the contents this time, and without hesitation quaffed the *mescal* to the last drop. He looked up. If ponies can smile, Conejo did so now, and foolishly too, rolled his eyes and wiggled his ears at the same time. Then, as if stung by a wasp, he bolted, kicked the air and ran away to the nearest brush. All day long he was heard running and snorting. At dusk he returned slowly, a sober horse, his colthood days behind him.

Next day, Juan José, seeing the sadness in his eyes, and knowing how it felt to have a *cruda* (hangover), offered him the bottle he always carried in his hip pocket.

"You need it, Conejo," he told the horse, "but just a little this time—two drinks—three drinks—and plenty of cold water." The horse, seeming to understand what his master was telling him, drank two swigs—three swigs—and then swallowed enough water to float his own body.

From that day on Conejo took his daily drink of *mescal,* and he was none the worse for it. In fact, it made him a horse of reputation. Other smugglers came to see him drink, and all admired him. "He should be called *El Pájaro Azul*," suggested one of the smugglers, noticing his fondness for that particular brand of *mescal.* And so El Pájaro he became now, little knowing that the name so glibly given would become a by-word among the people of the borderland.

A new relationship developed between El Pájaro and Juan José, one of respect and mutual admiration. But there was something he missed, the close contact with man, which only comes to a horse when he is ridden by his master. The children were no longer allowed to ride him; Juan José still laughed at his queer shape and thought him unworthy of riding. Every day, after his customary drink, he ran off like a flash of lighting to the brush, where he remained—unmolested—until the effects of the *mescal* left him.

Time passed for master and horse in this manner, and then on the feast day of Santiago, the patron saint of horses, Juan José, feeling unusually gay after their daily drink, said to El Pájaro, "*Pájaro,* I am going to ride you; you are to be my horse." And without more ado, he jumped on the unsuspecting horse. The struggle that followed was one of endurance—Pájaro trying to throw his master down, Juan José to hold on. At last, each recognizing the stubbornness and tenacity of the other, both stopped from sheer exhaustion.

The following day word came that a load of tobacco leaf and *mescal* was ready to be brought across the river. Calling his men together, Juan José planned the expedition for the first night after the last quarter of the moon, which would be four days hence.

El Pájaro was made ready for the expedition. He did not mind the saddle at all; and the bridle merely gave him a ticklish sensuous sensation in his mouth. Under cover of darkness Juan José and his men met at the river.

"*¡Vamos, Pájaro! Adentro,*" the rider whispered in his ear. Horse and rider plunged into the stream and swarm to the other side. The hidden load of smuggled goods was found; the mules were packed, and the smugglers again plunged into the river.

Land was reached in safety. Juan José was whispering commands into his horse's ear, but Pájaro was sniffing the air.

"*Ya, ya, Pájaro,*" whispered Juan José. "Keep quiet, steady."

Unheeding his master's words and caresses, Pájaro reared on his powerful, short hind legs and without warning fled to the chaparral. Hardly had he brought his master to the safety of the brush when the Rangers fell upon the smugglers, wounding some and taking the rest under their custody.

Because of this incident, Pájaro's fame as a "Ranger sniffler" spread over the borderland. Fleet as a rabbit, with the intelligence of his Arabian father and the endurance of his plebeian mother, he was the envy of all the *rancheros.* Fabulous sums of money were offered for this *mescal*-drinking horse, but Juan José would not sell him. He was too valuable to the smuggler; with this aid, Juan José and his men became unconquerable.

However, with the development of the lower Rio Grande Valley, swift changes came to the border. Smuggling became unprofitable. No longer did it pay the smugglers to bring in fresh supplies of tobacco leaf. Bull Durham and brown paper was taking place of the corn shuck *cigarrillos.* No longer was it spectacular to swim the river under the very nose of the Texas Rangers. For these officers, seeing the demand for tobacco diminish, directed their activities to more active sources. And without the thrill of persecution smuggling lost all zest and glamour. Juan José, who always liked to occupy the center of the stage, did a dramatic thing then. Repenting his sinful life, he acquired religion and decided to lead the life of a saint. It was then that he sold El Pájaro, the wonder horse. A rich *ranchero,* Don Manuel de Guevara, became his new master. Juan José wept over his horse at parting, begging Don Manuel not to give him any more *mescal.*

"He is part of my very soul," Juan José explained. "With my repentance came his too. He is as much of a Christian as I am."

But with the new master and the new life, El Pájaro lost spirit. His eyes lost luster, he refused to eat, and when saddled merely stood still. His new master cursed and swore, saying he had been cheated in the bargain. Then like a flash a thought came into his mind. The horse needed *mescal.* And he was right. A quart of the fiery liquid restored the horse to his former manner. El Pájaro pitched and snorted as of old. He became so spirited that no one, except the *ranchero,* could ride him. A man in his early forties, Don Manuel was the typical *ranchero* of his time. A good *jinete,* he bragged that no horse could throw him and no rider could outride him. And to a certain extent the boast was true. Except when he was "in the grape," the polite border way of saying he was drunk, he could ride any horse. He used to boast that if Pegasus himself, the fabulous winged horse, were placed before him, he could ride him—wings and all. El Pájaro had met his match.

In those days, at the turn of the nineteenth century, there was no better known figure than Father José María. A native of France, he had come to the border country as a young man of twenty-five, forty years before. Because of his excellent horsemanship, he was lovingly known as the "Cowboy Priest." Now as an aging man of sixty-five, he still rode all over the lower border administering the sacraments and preaching the gospel. Loved and respected by all, his word was law among a people who had very little liking and less respect for American law.

One evening, just at sunset, Father José María, riding his white mule, arrived at Don Manuel's ranch. Hearing the cries of a woman, the hoarse swearing of a man, and the weeping of children, he entered the yard of the ranch house without announcing himself. The sight that met his eyes did not surprise him at all, for he knew Don Manuel only too well.

The *ranchero* was much "in grape" and so was El Pájaro. Don Manuel could hardly stand on his feet; yet he was trying to ride the snorting and pitching horse. His wife stood on the porch wringing her hands and weeping. The children were adding to their wails and tears to hers, and the two peons standing against the house were paralyzed with fear. Don Manuel would surely be killed if he succeeded in getting on El Pájaro.

Father José María took in the scene at a glance. Dismounting from his mule, he came to where Manuel struggled with El Pájaro, "*Hola Padre,*" the *ranchero* called out, "watch me ride this devil of a horse."

"Stop a moment, Manuelito," answered the priest. "I'll make a bet with you."

Manuel stopped, for if there was a thing he loved more than *mescal* and horses, it was to make and win an honest bet.

"A bet, *Padre,* did you say?"

"Yes, I bet I can ride El Pájaro."

"All right, *Padre.* I take your bet. If you ride this demon of a horse, he is yours. Agreed?" "Agreed," the priest answered.

With slow steps the priest approached the horse—caressed him gently, patting his mane and rubbing his nose. In less time than any one realized, Father José María was riding El Pájaro. The *mescal*-drinking horse and the *mescal*-drinking *ranchero* had been defeated.

From that time on El Pájaro was the priest's property. Years passed. The black-robed, white haired priest, learned in Latin, and the gentle, queer-shaped horse, *Stella Matutina* now, *alias El Conejo, alias El Pájaro,* traversed the borderland, bringing consolation to the sick and afflicted. Whenever the good priest talked to some impenitent sinner, he would often comment, "My horse, Morning Star, is a good example of what religion can do for a man. Imitate him. He has left his evil ways."

Tales of Humans

Tío Patricio

Every evening at dusk Tío Patricio was announced by the bleating of his unruly flock, which arrived enveloped in a cloud of dust. He was a giant dressed in a discarded soldier's uniform; however, his shoes and hat did not match his military array, for the former were rawhide *guaraches*[†] and the latter a high, pointed, broad-brimmed Mexican felt *sombrero*. His black patriarchal beard contrasted with his cheeks, rosy and firm like a girl's. In fact, his complexion was the envy of all the marriageable girls of the country side. Not seldom a *señorita* braver than the rest ventured to ask, "What do you wash your face with, Tío?"

The reply was always the same, "God's water," meaning rain water. And in that semi-arid part of the country rain is rare, three or four times a year at the most.

But that is another story.

You remember there was something peculiar about Tío Patricio. He always wore a hat in summer, in winter, in fair weather and foul. Even at night he slept with it over his face so as to cover his head. He was rather sensitive about it too; no sooner would one of the ranch hands mention the word *head* or *hair* than the *pastor* silently disappeared. Of course, every one wondered at this eccentricity but no one dared ask him to explain it. The most

Jovita González, "Tales and Songs of the Texas-Mexicans," *Man, Bird and Beast,* ed. J. Frank Dobie (Austin: Folk-Lore Society, 1932) 88-92.
[†]Rawhide sandals.

uncouth *vaquero* knows that no gentleman ever asks another anything concerning his personal appearance.

Sometime in November the master was to ship cattle, and new *vaqueros* were hired to help gather them. There was one in the outfit whom no one liked; he had snake-like beady black eyes that were as sly and as crafty as a coyote's. Probably this started the men calling him "Coyote."

One evening, as customary, we were sitting around the kitchen fire telling yarns and singing. This particular night "Coyote" was telling about the ghosts that haunt El Blanco ranch. "Just about this time," he concluded in a haunting voice, "the moon shone from behind a cloud and I noticed that the ghost was as hairless as a pumpkin."

At this Tío Patricio jumped as if he had been stung by a scorpion and shout out of the kitchen with the rapidity of a hare when pursued by hounds.

"What's wrong with him?" asked Coyote. "He is a queer steer, isn't he? And, tell me, why does he always wear that steeple-like structure on his head? Do you dare me to ask him why he never takes it off? I bet my *reata* against yours I'll do it. Who'll take my bid?"

No one said a word. Pancho changed the subject, for no one would hurt Tío Patricio's feelings willingly. We heard him fixing his bed in the bunk house. A mean look came into Coyote's eyes and I knew he meant to carry out his threat at the first opportunity.

"Come, boys," I said. "It is time to sleep. We have a hard day's work before us in the pasture tomorrow."

As we entered the house I saw Tío Patricio in bed with his hat over his face. Coyote went towards him.

"*Amigo,* you have forgotten to take off your hat." No answer. "I say, why don't you take it off, or shall I do it for you?"

He would have done it, too, had not Pancho grabbed him by the arm.

"Can't you see he is asleep," said Pancho, "and, what is more, you leave him alone. Do you hear?"

All expected trouble. Coyote measured Pancho with his eyes and, seeing the muscles of his arms and the determination on his face, skulked away.

Before daylight Tío Patricio was up and could be heard calling his dog in the corral. Not one word did any one say about last night's episode, all hoping that Coyote would forget about it.

"I tell you what we'll do," he said next morning as we were coming to the mess house for breakfast. "Suppose we recite the Rosary during the month of December; I am not much for religion but during this time I feel the need of it in my heart."

Although much surprised at the suggestion, all assented willingly, and I felt somewhat ashamed of my ill feelings towards him, and right then and there I made up my mind to like him.

Tío Patricio was not there during the services and all were surprised. He was not an overzealous religious man but we all knew his love and devotion for the Virgin.

Two weeks before Christmas Coyote suggested we have *Las Posadas.* As every one knows, these are the most solemn and beautiful services of the Christmas season. It is a service which we who are still Christians and speak God's own language hold every year in honor of the birth of the Christ Child.

"Since there is no church and no regular choir," continued Coyote, "I am going to ask the master to lend us a statue of the Virgin and we can have the services outside. You men will be arranged in groups so you can sing better; and other group representing Joseph and Mary go about asking for shelter and are refused everywhere. The person or group nearest the Virgin will take them in and with that the celebration will close."

"Can any one as repulsive looking as this man be capable of such beautiful ideas?" thought I. We were so busy rehearsing our hymns that we forgot all about Tío Patricio. All this time he had kept away from us and I noticed he looked worried. Probably, it was suggested, the goats were not doing so well this winter or he had lost some kids.

Christmas Eve finally came. About eight we went to the *portal,* the place of the celebration. Every man conscious of his new shirt and rather sensitive about it, took his appointed seat. At a signal the first group arose, went to the improvised altar, and sang the introduction:

Esta noche caballeros	This night gentlemen,
Es Noche de Navidad	Is Christmas Eve.
Parió la Virgen María	The Virgin Mary gave birth
Parió en humilde portal.	Under an humble roof.

The first group representing the holy Pilgrims started their pilgrimage:

Es José y María	This is Joseph and Mary,
Su esposa amada	His beloved wife;
Es José y María	This is Joseph and Mary
pidiendo posada.	Asking for shelter.

To which the addressed replied:

Mi casa es pequeña	My house is very small
No caben en ella.	There is no room for all.

And thus we went the rounds of all the groups. All this time I had been wondering who was to give lodging to the Pilgrims. Then my eyes fell on Tío Patricio. The man sat rigid, pale as the moon outside. On his face was the look of a haunted beast. And then it all dawned on me. He was to sing the verse of acceptance. And he had to kneel bareheaded before the Virgin's altar. I knew

Coyote was a despicable skunk, but I had not dreamed he would dare do a thing like this.

By this time all eyes were fixed on Tío Patricio. May I die before I again see any one looking so abject and terrified. Have you ever seen a rabbit which, charmed by a snake, knows that soon it is to be devoured? That is the way Tío Patricio's looked. I glanced towards Coyote; the grin of triumph on his ugly face made his namesake look handsome.

The time came for Tío Patricio to sing. He got up and, walking with the steps of a somnambulist, approached the altar.

He knelt and took off his hat.

He was bald.

A dry hoarse sob shook his mighty frame.

We left him there with his humiliation alone with the mother of God.

Tío Patricio's interpretation of the stars was accepted by the whole countryside. Thus the Milky Way is the path of the saints; in June it is the trail through which St. John ascended to heaven; in July it is the path of the apostles Peter and Paul, while in August it is St. James who traverses the heavens on his white steed. Caster and Pollux are the eyes of Lucy, the little Roman maid who preferred blindness to man's love. The eyes which she lost in her struggle for chastity are up there in the southern sky to serve as a warning to frivolous maidens. Farther down the heavens are the three bright stars, Orion, or the three Marys— Mary the mother, Mary Magdalene, and Mary the sister of Martha—who keep watch over Lucy's eyes. Venus, the morning star, is the Virgin who wakes the shepherds at dawn.

More vivid in detail and coloring are Tío Patricio's stories of birds. Every one in Texas is familiar with the road-runner, the Nemesis of rattlesnakes. This bird is commonly known as the *paisano*. The term is wrongly applied, for in its literal sense it means *countryman,* and is a corruption of the word *faisán,* pheasant, to which family the road-runner is wrongly supposed to belong. It really belongs to the cuckoo family. Whether *paisano, faisán* or road-runner, the legend connected with it is the same.

Juan, *el Loco*

"*Vive Dios,*" said the driver of the coach; "may the earth swallow me alive, if the man walking towards us is not the very person I am in search of."

The speaker was a middle-aged, stalwart Mexican gentleman—a Texas ranchman who with his family was going to the nearest town across the river in search of a much needed *pastor.*

"Marcos," continued the ranchman, addressing his Mexican outrider, "you ride ahead and bring the man to me, while I drive the coach under the shade of that mesquite tree over there."

The *peón* soon returned, with the man some twenty feet behind.

"He is a queer man, Don Francisco. He talks as though he smoked marihuana."

"I am sure that the goats don't care about that, and neither do I. What I am interested in is that he seems to have the makings of an excellent *pastor.*"

"*Amigo,*" went on Don Francisco, turning to the man who had followed the *peón,* "would you like to work for me? I'll pay you fifteen dollars a month and all you can eat."

"Aha!" answered the stranger. "You are the big burly witch-man who drives a coach pulled by four white mules and rides his witches along."

Jovita González, "Among My People," *Southwest Review* Jan. 1932: 179-181.

And that is how Juan el Loco made his appearance in the border ranches some thirty years ago. He was surrounded by mystery. Not even his name was known; in lieu of a better one he was generally known by the sobriquet of John the Mad. He was of medium height, fair but with dark eyes and hair. In spite of his wanderings on foot, he was always clean. All his worldly possessions consisted of a comb and a piece of broken mirror. But on his arrival at a ranch the first thing he did was to ask for a change of old clothes. After bathing at the *aguaje*, he would return clean and refreshed and invite himself to sit down at the kitchen table. He always made himself handy around the house by carrying wood and water, feeding the chickens, and playing with the children, among whom he was a great favorite. All attempts to find out something about his family or his home were futile. When he was questioned on the subject, his answer was some crazy remark about how the witches were always with him urging him to go on. It was said by the *vaqueros* and the *rancheros* that he became worse on Fridays and when the moon was full. On those days he went into trances, and the witches undoubtedly visited him then, for armed with a club he gesticulated and struck the air, always addressing the evil spirits in the most profane language. The next day he would be peaceful again, worn out and exhausted from his ordeal.

Time has passed since then. The old-time *rancheros* have now sold or leased their ranches and Juan el Loco does not feel at home among the new owners. No longer does he wander through the ranches; he has made his headquarters in the town of Roma. He is now an old man, but the witches still hold him. And he wanders yet from house to house doing his accustomed chores, carrying water and wood and feeding the chickens.

Don José María

Don José María was one of the richest landowners of the lower Rio Grande valley. He had more cattle, more horses, more mules, and more goats and sheep than any other *ranchero.* In his pretentious stone house, square and flat-roofed, he lived like a feudal lord, ever in readiness to receive friends and foes. A warm welcome awaited his friends; a hot and exciting one, his enemies. Monotonous and uninteresting from the outside, his home was the center of border culture—not the culture of Mexico, not the culture of the United States, but a culture peculiar to the community.

A tyrant by temperament, Don José María was feared and respected by all who knew him. If he appeared in the corral riding his powerful black horse, his eyebrows contracted in a frown, one higher than the other, the stoutest *vaquero* trembled in his boots. Don José's expression was the sign of a tempest that would soon hurl itself with the fury of a tropical tornado. His word was law, and as he rode through his possessions lashing the *vaqueros* with his tongue, and not seldom with his *reata,* no one dared utter a word. But though he was the lord of many, he was the slave of one—Doña Margarita, his wife. And as he thundered through the rooms of his vast house, his spurs echoing on the cement floors, one look from his wife was sufficient to calm him.

Jovita González, "Among My People," *Southwest Review* Jan. 1932: 181-184.

"José María, my lamb, let me read to you a while." Then the lion, now a lamb indeed, would sit by her side while she read to him from the lives of the saints, *Romeo and Juliet,* or some romantic novel. For Doña Margarita was a well-read woman whose specialty was Spanish versions of French and English love stories. She played the organ and the accordion, and when her reading was not sufficient to soothe Don José María, she played to him melodies that both had loved in their youth. Doña Margarita was the undisputed mistress of her home, her eleven children, and the women of the ranch. Every evening the ranch people gathered in the big *sala* to hear music from the phonograph or stories from Doña Margarita. The gatherings always ended with evening prayers, led by the mistress of the house. These were always punctuated by commands or reproofs:

"Hail Mary, full of grace—José María, you are nodding, my love. The Lord is with thee—Felipe, stop tickling your sister. Blessed art thou amongst women—José María, I heard you snore. . . ."

And so it went.

Like all Mexicans of their class, both Don José and Doña Margarita were devout Catholics, and the coming of the missionary priest was the occasion to display border magnificence and hospitality. People from the adjoining ranches came, the landowners as well as the *vaqueros* and servants. Preparations for the event were made days in advance. Bread and cakes were baked; cocoa beans were roasted and ground and made into chocolate squares; a cow or a calf was butchered; hens were dressed; and the unused quilts and mattresses were aired. The servant quarters were astir with excitement. The girls looked forward to getting a new sweetheart; the boys anxiously anticipated seeing new girls. Servant women were kept busy grinding corn on the *metate* for *tortillas,* while others washed the linen to be used for the altar.

Those homemade altars were the joy and pride of feminine art. At one end of the *sala* a sheet was hung to the wall; and on it were constructed with varicolored ribbons, red, yellow, orange, and blue, arches and arcades that would have made any architect blush with envy. Sprays of cedar and oleander and artificial flowers were pinned here and there, making the already impossible arches more impossible still. Pictures of saints and angels formed a celestial host, and holy statues, some of wood and some of marble, were placed on the altar table.

At twilight, while the people were still arriving, the priest told his beads as he walked up and down the *patio*. After supper all came to the improvised altar to recite the rosary and hear a sermon. After each decade of the rosary, the hoarse voices of the *vaqueros* and servants would mingle with the tenor of some ranch singer and the voice of the women and children in praises to the mother of God:

O María, Madre Mía	[O Mary, our mother,
Consuelo del mortal,	Consolation of mortals,
Amparadme y guiadme	Protect us and guide us
A la patria celestial.	To our celestial home.]

Both Don José María and his wife spent their money recklessly. Syrian peddlers made special trips from San Antonio to the San Juan ranch, and Doña Margarita's boast was that after the peddlers had been to her home, they did not have to go anywhere else. To be different from their neighbors, she and Don José María ordered their groceries by catalogue from Sears Roebuck.

The coming of the automobile was a disaster; for just as each of the three unmarried daughters had a piano, so each one of the five unmarried sons must have a car.

The only occasion when Don José María could not be controlled by his wife was when one of his daughters married. Like all fathers of Latin stock, he hated to see his daughters leave the paternal home. When each one married, he would leave the ranch suicide bound. Armed with a pistol, a knife, a rope, and poison, he would escape to the nearest *potrero* determined to end his life in one way or another. But each time he would return late in the evening after the last guest had departed.

"José María, my love, you are an idiot," Doña Margarita would greet him.

"I know it, my pearl," Don José María would reply meekly. And with that, taking his whip, he would mount his black horse and ride away like lightning.

Don Tomás

O n the ground was a youth, semi-naked, his back and chest crossed with thick welts from which blood steamed. Above him towered a lean, gray-headed giant, rawhide rope in hand, beating the prostate form mercilessly. With a cry of anguish and pain, the youth staggered from the ground, only to fall back in a faint. Seeing this, the older man gathered the blood-covered form of the youth gently in his arms, took him indoors, and laid him on a cot. In a corner of the room three weeping women huddled together. The oldest of the group fell on her knees in front of the cot, kissed the pale face of the youth, and cried in an anguished voice,

"Tomás, you have killed our son!"

"No," the man replied proudly, "I have merely taught him not to steal cattle again. Bring water and salve and I'll dress his wounds."

Such was patriarchal justice among the Mexican *rancheros* of the border land. The stern father was Don Tomás, a well known character of the border country. Materially, Don Tomás was not a rich man. In the center of his few thousand acres of brush-covered land and near a stream was his home, a big, thatch-covered *jacal.* Close by, separated by a *portal,* another *jacal* served as kitchen and dining room. And beyond, near the stream, were the *corrales* for his cows and goats.

Jovita González, "Among My People," *Southwest Review* Jan. 1932: 184-187.

He believed in parental dominion. He was head of his family. His word was authority; no other law was needed and there was no necessity for civil interference. He was the sole judge of his children's actions, whether they were married or single.

His ranch was near my grandfather's, and although he did not belong to what was considered the landed gentry, he and my grandfather were the best of friends and *compadres.*[†] My earliest recollection of Don Tomás is of seeing him ride up on a spirited *bayo potro,* descend from it with a leap, and tie it to a salt cedar tree by the gate. Although he was a *texano,* he dressed like a Mexican *ranchero,* always in brown, with a black silk sash around his waist, a bright-colored *sarape* over one shoulder, and a Mexican *sombrero* in his head. He was tall and slender, and in spite of his sixty-odd years was the champion wrestler of the community. I remember him well as he would walk arrogantly about, his silver spurs clinking on the brick floor of the patio. His lean face with its gray, pointed beard was striking because of the clear-cut features and deep-set gray eyes. What as a child I used to think were blue freckles were grains of gunpowder from a shotgun that had once exploded in his hands.

He knew more about setting bones, treating snake bites, and curing sunstroke than any other man in the region. He applied the same cures to man and beast, and his boast was that he had never lost a patient. A strip of deerskin tied around the victim's neck, for instance, would cure any one of a snake bite. But although Don Tomás might cure any disease or wound, there was one thing which was beyond him—witchcraft. And this was the cause of the ruin and disintegration of his family and his patriarchal rule.

All of his married sons lived on his ranch. And if little birds in their own nest can not agree, neither can sisters-in-law. The

---

[†]The godfather of a child is called *compadre* by the child's father. The relationship is a very close family tie.

quarrel started when one daughter-in-law accused the child of another of having stolen a ring. After much bickering and quarreling, the offended party swore that some day all concerned would be sorry for the insult she and her child had suffered.

Some time later, when the families were gathered together at Don Tomás's house in the evening, a shrill whistle broke the stillness of the twilight. It was a screech owl, the bird of ill omen, the messenger of the witches.

Things happened after that. Don Tomás's wife was the first to be stricken. She was bewitched and went insane. The next day a daughter went raving mad, and was taken to the county jail for safe keeping. One of the sons imagined himself a cat, crawled on all fours, lapped milk from a saucer, and perched himself on the beam of a house. Another one became a general, rallied the ranch children together, and drilled them all day in military fashion. Worst of all, a second daughter was possessed of the Evil Spirit, who attempted to strangle her in the darkness of the night. Next day her neck and face were bruised and showed the marks that the Evil One had left. The food prepared for the stricken turned to worms, and the fruits from a can of peaches that was opened one day became stones. Exotic flowers, never seen before at the ranch, were placed in vases about the house.

One day, a Friday to be exact, the bewitched became worse and a shower of ashes fell upon the place, killing all growing things. Even the dogs went blind and staggered about the place in a most pitiable manner. That night the daughter in jail died, the other was strangled, and Pancho, perched on the beam, mewed in the most terrifying manner, while screech owls held a concert over the roof. A priest who was called blessed the ranch and spoke to Don Tomás in strong terms about the nonexistence of witchcraft.

"You may know a great deal about religion, *padre*, but you know nothing about the witches."

And evidently the good *padre* did not, for when a *curandero* was called, this was his decree: all had been bewitched by a member of the family, and the welfare of all concerned depended upon the death of the sorceress. The daughter-in-law's threat was remembered, and every one believed she was the guilty person.

One of Don Tomás's sons, crazed by his fear of the evil spirits and athirst to avenge the sufferings of his family, took it upon himself to release them from the evil influences that possessed them. Early the following morning he went to his sister-in-law's house and while she was still in bed stabbed her seven times with a *machete.*

After the incident the three remaining patients regained their health, but the liberator of the family was given a life sentence.

I went to the border a few months after the event and made it a point to visit Don Tomás. He was a broken man. His son's disgrace and the misfortunes of his family had crushed his proud spirit.

"That's American law," he said, shaking his fist at his imaginary enemy. "It does away with paternal discipline. It tears your heart and disgraces an honorable name. I could have dealt with my youngest as I did with my eldest years ago."

My stay at the ranch was brief. I could not stand the atmosphere of dread that permeated the place. Don Tomás told me such harrowing tales of the supernatural, of the occult power of the witches, that when at night the owls called to each other I imagined myself in the clutches of some evil spirit. And so I left.

Pedro The Hunter

Pedro was a wonderful person among all the people in the ranch. Besides being the most renowned hunter, he had seen the world, and, conscious of his superiority, he strutted among the *vaqueros* and other ranch hands like an only rooster in a small barnyard. Besides, he spoke English, which he had learned on one of his trips up North. Yes, Pedro was a traveled man: he had been as far away as Sugar Land and had worked in the sugar cane plantation. Many strange things he had seen in his travels. He had seen how the convicts were worked on the plantations and how they were whipped for the least offense. Yes, he, Pedro, had seen that with his own eyes.

There was something strange that he could not understand. Not all Americans were white. He had seen some as black as coal, who had wool for hair and big, thick purple lips. He had gone to one of their dances, but had not been able to stay long. They smelled like buzzards. The odor was so strong he could hear it. No, he was not mistaken; he was sure they were Americans. Did they not speak English? He did not stay in the Sugar Land country long; the dampness was making him have chills. So he hired himself as a section hand. His auditors should have seen that big black monster, *el Tren Volador.* It roared and whis-

Jovita González, "Among My People," *Tone the Bell Easy,* ed. J. Frank Dobie (Austin: Texas Folk-Lore Society,1932) 101-102. This story was republished in *Mexican American Authors,* eds. Américo Paredes and Raymundo Paredes (Boston: Houghton-Mifflin, 1972) 10-11.

tled and belched fire and smoke as it flew over the land. He would have liked being a section hand on the railroads had it not been for the food—cornbread and salt pork.

He had been told that if he ate salt pork he would soon learn to speak English. Bah! What a lie! He had eaten it three times a day and had only learned to say "yes." But, being anxious to see a city, he came to Houston. As he walked through the down-town streets one Saturday evening he saw some beautiful American ladies singing at the corner. What attracted his attention was that they played the guitar. And that made him homesick for the ranch. He stopped to listen, and the beautiful ladies talked to him and patted him on the back. They took him with them that night and let him sleep in a room above the garage. He could not understand them, but they were very kind and taught him to play the drum, and every evening the ladies, after putting on a funny hat, took the guitars and he the drum, and they went to town. They sang beautifully, and he beat the drum in a way that must have caused the envy of the passersby, and when he passed a plate, many people put money in it. During the winter he learned English. But with the coming of spring he got homesick for the *mesquitales,* the fragrant smell of the *huisache,* the lowing of cattle at sundown, and, above all, for the mellow, rank smell of the corral. What would he not give for a good cup of black, strong ranch coffee, and a piece of jerky broiled over the fire! And so one night, with his belongings wrapped up in a blanket, he left south by west for the land of his youth. And here he was again, a man who had seen the world but who was happy to be at home.

The Mail Carrier

No people of the North feel cold more than do the border people when the winter norther sweeps down. In the teeth of one of these northers we left Las Víboras ranch just before dawn, bound for the nearest railroad station, Hebbronville. The day proved to be as dreary as the dawn, and I amused myself counting the stiff jack rabbits that crossed our path. At a turn of the road the car almost collided with a forlorn-looking two-wheeled vehicle drawn by the sorriest-looking nag I had ever seen. On the high seat, perched like a bright-colored tropical bird, sat a figure wrapped up in a crazy quilt. On seeing us, he stopped, motioned us to do the same, and in mumbled tones bade us good morning, asked where we were going, what might be the news at the ranches, and, finally, were we all right. He seemed to ask these questions for the sake of asking, not waiting for reply to any one of them. At last, having paused in his catechism long enough for some sort of reply to be given, he put out one of his hands gingerly from under his brilliant cape to wave us good-bye.

"That's Tío Esteban, the mail carrier, grandfather said. And that is how I met this employee of Uncle Sam. Six months later, suitcase and all, I rode with him twenty miles as a passenger, for the sum of two dollars and fifty cents. That summer we became

Jovita González, "Among My People," *Tone the Bell Easy,* ed. J. Frank Dobie (Austin: Texas Folk-Lore Society, 1932) 102-104. This story was republished in *Mexican American Authors,* eds. Américo Paredes and Raymund Paredes (Boston: Houghton-Mifflin, 1972) 11-12.

intimate friends. He was the weather-beaten, brown-faced, black-eyed Cupid of the community. Often when some lovesick *vaquero* did not have a two-cent stamp to pay for the delivery of the love missive, he personally delivered the letter. Not only did he carry letters, but also he served as secretary to those who could not write. He possessed a wonderful memory and could recite ballads and love poems by the hour. If the amorous outburst was in verse, his fee was double. He was a sly old fellow and knew all the love affairs of the community. I am not so sure of his honorableness as a mail carrier. I am afraid he sometimes opened the love missives. Once as he handed a love letter to Serafina, our cook, he said in a mellifluous voice, "My dear Serafina, as the poet says, we are like two cooing doves." Poor Serafina blushed even to the white of her eyes. Later she showed me that very phrase in the letter.

Tío Esteban knew not only all the love affairs but also all the scandal of the two counties through which he passed. And because of that, he was the welcome guest of every ranch house. He made grandfather's house his headquaters and could always have a bed with the ranch hands. He needed little encouragement to begin talking. He usally sat in a low stool, cleared his throat, and went through all the other preliminaries of a long-winded speaker. Ah, how we enjoyed his news! What did he care for what the papers said? They told of wars in Europe, of thousands of boys killed in the trenches, of political changes, of the Kaiser's surrender. But what was all this compared to what Tío Esteban had to tell us?

Did we know Chon had left his wife becase she didn't wash her face often enough? And about Felipe's hog eating all the soap his wife had made? Pablo's setting hen, which had all white Leghorn eggs, had hatched all black chickens. A strange event, but not so strange if you remembered that Pablo's sister-in-law had black chickens. And with such news he entertained us until the roosters began to crow.

The Perennial Lover

Las hijas de las	"The daughters of the
madres que amé tanto	mothers I loved so well
me besan ya como	They kiss me now as
se besa un santo.	they would kiss a saint."

Carlitos had made love to two generations of girls. As one crop of girls grew up to maidenhood, Carlitos declared his sentiments to each in turn. One by one they outgrew him, married and had girls of their own. As the second crop came on, he remained ever-ready to offer his heart and hand to anyone who would listen to him.

He was not bad looking. He was tall and lanky, and had it not been for his coconut head, pivoted on some eight inches of neck, his triangular ears, and big hands and splay feet, he would have been handsome. His mustache was the barometer for his emotions. When he was not in love it hung limp and unkept, but in the spring, when the world was aglow with prairie flowers and all Nature invited him to love, it was waxed and triumphant. I remember his coming to the ranch one day and calling my uncle aside most mysteriously.

"Look, Francisco," he said, displaying a package of ruled paper, with carnations on one corner, "beautiful, isn't it? This year the carnations are bound to work. Last year I used violets

Jovita González, "Among My People," *Tone The Bell Easy,* ed. J. Frank Dobie (Austin: Texas Folk-Lore Society, 1932) 104-105. This story was republished in *Mexican American Authors,* eds. Américo Paredes and Raymund Paredes (Boston: Houghton-Mifflin,1972) 13-14.

and did not get a single answer. That's because violets do not inspire love; but wait until they see these carnations. I will get so many replies that it will be difficult for me to decide which girl I want. And look! This is what I am going to say."

Then he showed my uncle the circular which he sent every year, his declaration of love, for he always used the same, whether he sent it by mail or uttered it, one hand over his heart and eyes looking up to heaven for inspiration: "I can no longer bear the pain which devours my heart, and I will like to know whether my love is returned or not. Should I be so unfortunate as to be rejected, then I will put between us the immensity of the sea." But in spite of many rejections and more ignorings, he never left on his threatened voyages. He might for a few days go about in a mood suitable to a rejected lover, but he soon forgot.

One May, not long ago, I was back at the ranch and in the store when Carlitos entered. He was the most dejected-looking figure imaginable; his once beautiful mustache was the most melancholy part about him. Between sighs he told the clerk what he wanted. With another sigh he left the store. "What's the matter with him?" I asked my uncle. "Caught at last," he answered with a laugh. "Last spring, as usual, he distributed his love letters, and, much to his antonishment, he was accepted by Lola, Tío Felipe's thirty-year-old daughter. When he opened the letter, I though he had received a death notice. He turned as pale as a ghost, and I had to hold him up. When he had somewhat recovered, he said to me in choking voice, "Look, look." I looked and read, "I am greatly honored by your offer, which I'm happy to accept with my father's consent."

"I must congratulate you upon your good fortune," I said, offering my hand. "But you do not understand," he said between sobs. "I never meant to marry at all. I merely sent those letters because it gave me pleasure. Whatever shall I do in the spring now?"

And this was spring, and his first year of married life.

Tío Pancho Malo

Tío Pancho Malo, they called him. After the fashion of these simple Mexican folk, the surname originated, not from the fact that he was bad, but from the fact that he was different. No, he was not bad. He merely had his own queer notions, his own ideas which he followed in his own peculiar way. And unconformity with the general tendencies and general customs is sufficient to make anyone an outlaw amid any group of simple folk.

Tío Pancho was a philosopher, and, like all philosophers, he was at outs with the world and his fellow men. I knew him as an old toothless, wizened creature, weak physically, but mentally sharp and alert. He spoke very little then. But, as I went to the border country, I would often hear, "as Tío Pancho Malo did," or "as Tío Pancho Malo said." If he himself was not willing to speak, those who knew him were only too glad to tell you, and always with a laugh, concerning the old man and his idiosyncrasies.

As a young married man, he had lived near Mier, in Mexico, on his few ancestral acres of worthless alkaline land. "Bitter mesquites and poor folks' children are plentiful," is an old border saying. And Tío Pancho's flock was more plentiful than the mesquite beans. His boys never bothered about keeping clean, for during the first two years of their life they were miniature

Jovita González, "Among My People," *Tone the Bell Easy,* ed. J. Frank Dobie. (Austin: Texas Folk-Lore Society, 1932) 105-108. This story was republished in *Mexican American Authors,* eds. Américo Paredes and Raymund Paredes (Boston: Houghton-Mifflin, 1972) 14-16.

Adams—except they wore no fig leaves—in a place far from being a Garden of Eden. When rebuked because of this indecency he permitted, he replied in a drawling voice, "Why should I interfere with the plans of my Creator? If He wanted children to wear clothes, He in His goodness would provide them."

When his wife died, she was buried without a coffin. "Who am I," he explained, "that I should prevent Nature from fulfilling her end? The sooner she mingles with Mother Earth, the sooner her destiny is fulfilled." After his wife's death, he and his boys moved to Texas, where he became a *pastor* of goats. When the flock did not demand too much attention, he planted a few acres of land. One day it is said the ranch people were driven to hysterics by the appearance of his boys wearing gourds for hats.

"What is the object of a hat?" he asked. "Is it not protection from the elements? There in the shape of a gourd Nature has provided us with something that serves the same purpose and that does not cost anything."

He could neither read nor write; yet he composed poetry and expressed himself in a most flowery language. One day when he wanted an axe he commanded one of his sons to bring him "that bright shiny object which man in his cruelty uses for the decapitation of defenseless trees."

When his boys grew up, his great exploit was the organization of a band. He did not know any music; neither did his sons. However, what difference did that make? Their instruments were of the most rudimentary forms; reed flutes, hand-made guitars, an old fife, a trombone, cymbals and a drum. As director, Tío Malo led this band from ranch to ranch, playing selections which they composed as the spirit moved them. Once they came to Grandfather's ranch, and a more raggedy bunch I have never seen. They played a few selections, at the end of which Grandfather asked them if they played by note.

"No," Tío Pancho Malo replied, "we play for chickens, beans, corn, or whatever the rancheros may have, but we never require a note."

He was very proud of his son's accomplishments as musicians, and often paid them compliments but never in their presence.

"My Tirso," he said confidentially to Grandfather, "plays the trombone with the strength of an ox."

Tío Pancho Malo went up and down the river playing his music and expounding his theories. As the years passed and the boys married off, the band disbanded and Tío Pancho was left alone. The last I heard of him he was at Alice, Texas, where he eked out a living as a water carrier. He was brought before the court by the society for the prevention of cruelty to animals, accused to having ill-treated his donkey.

"Your Honor," he told the judge, "these good ladies have accused me of cruelty toward my donkey, saying that I make the poor skinny creature work. But these ladies have not stopped to consider that I also am poor, skinny and have to work. The donkey and I live for each other. Without me he would starve; without him I would die of hunger. We work together, and for each other. One of us is not any good without the other. If these ladies prevent his working, both of us will starve, and that in my mind would not only be cruelty to animals but cruelty to me."

The court could do nothing but let Tío Pancho Malo go his way.

The Bullet-Swallower

He was a wiry little man, a bundle of nerves in perpetual motion. Quicksilver might have run through his veins instead of blood. His right arm, partly paralyzed as a result of a *machete* cut he had received in a saloon brawl, terminated in stiff, claw-like, dirty-nailed fingers. One eye was partly closed— a knife cut had done that—but the other, amber in color, had the alertness and the quickness of a hawk's. Chairs were not made for him. Squatting on the floor or sitting on one heel, he told interminable stories of border feuds, bandit raids and smuggler fights as he fingered a curved, murderous knife which ended in three inches of zigzag, jagged steel. "No one has ever escaped this," he would say, caressing it. "Sticking it into a man might not have finished him, but getting it out—ah, my friend, that did the work. It's a very old one, brought from Spain, I guess," he would add in an unconcerned voice. "Here is the date, 1630."

A landowner by inheritance, a trail driver by necessity, and a smuggler and gambler by choice, he had given up the traditions of his family to be and do that which pleased him most. Through some freakish mistake, he had been born three centuries too late. He might have been a fearless *conquistador,* or he might have been a chivalrous knight of the Rodrigo de Narváez type, fighting the infidels along the Moorish frontier. A tireless horseman, a man

González, Jovita. "The Bullet Swallower," *Puro México*. Ed. J. Frank Dobie. (Austin: Texas Folk-Lore Society, 1935); facsimile, (Dallas: Southern Methodist University Press, 1969) 107-114.

of *pelo en pecho* (hair on the chest), as he braggingly called himself, he was afraid of nothing.

"The men of my time were not lily-livered, white-gizzarded creatures," he would boast. "We fought for the thrill of it, and the sight of blood maddened us as it does a bull. Did we receive a gash on the stomach? Did the guts come out? What of it. We tightened our sash and continued the fray. See this arm? Ah, could it but talk, it would tell you how many men it sent to the other world. To Hell, perhaps to Purgatory, but none I am sure to Heaven. The men I associated with were neither sissies nor saints. Often at night when I can not sleep because of the pain in these cursed wounds, I say a prayer, in my way, for their souls, in case my prayers should reach the good God.

"People call me *Traga-Balas,* Bullet-Swallower—Antonio Traga-Balas, to be more exact. *Ay,* were I as young as I was when the incident that gave me this name happened!

"We were bringing several cartloads of smuggled goods to be delivered at once and in safety to the owner. Oh, no, the freight was not ours but we would have fought for it with our life's blood. We had dodged the Mexican officials, and now we had to deal with the Texas Rangers. They must have been tipped, because they knew the exact hour we were to cross the river. We swam in safety. The pack mules, loaded with packages wrapped in tanned hides, we led by the bridle. We hid the mules in a clump of *tules* and were just beginning to dress when the Rangers fell upon us. Of course, we did not have a stitch of clothes on; did you think we swam fully dressed? Had we but had our guns in readiness, there have might be a different story to tell. We would have fought like wild-cats to keep the smuggled goods from falling into their hands. It was not ethical among smugglers to lose the property of a Mexican to Americans, and as to falling ourselves into their hands, we preferred death a thousand times. It's no disgrace and dishonor to die like a man, but it is to die like a rat. Only canaries sing; men never tell, however tortured they may be. I have seen the Rangers pumping water into the mouth of an innocent man because he would not confess to something he had not done. But that is another story.

"I ran to where the pack mules were to get my gun. Like a fool that I was, I kept yelling at the top of my voice, "You so, so and so gringo cowards, why don't you attack men like men? Why do you wait until they are undressed and unarmed?" I must have said some very insulting things, for one of them shot at me right in the mouth. The bullet knocked all of my front teeth out, grazed my tongue and went right through the back of my neck. Didn't kill me though. It takes more than bullets to kill Antonio Traga-Balas. The next thing I knew I found myself in a shepherd's hut. I had been left for dead, no doubt, and I had been found by the goatherd. The others were sent to the penitentiary. After I recovered, I remained in hiding for a year or so; and when I showed myself all thought it a miracle that I had lived through. That's how I was rechristened Traga-Balas. That confounded bullet did leave my neck a little stiff; I can't turn around as easily as I should, but outside of that I am as fit as though the accident—I like to call it that—had never happened. It takes a lot to kill a man, at least one who can swallow bullets.

"I've seen and done many strange things in my life and I can truthfully say that I have never been afriad but once. What are bullets and knife thrusts to seeing a corpse arise from its coffin? Bullets can be dodged and dagger cuts are harmless unless they hit a vital spot. But a dead man staring with lifeless, open eyes and gaping mouth is enough to make a man tremble in his boots. And, mind you, I am not a coward, never have been. Is there any one among you who thinks Antonio Traga-Balas is a coward?"

At a question like this, Traga-Balas would take the knife from its cover and finger it in a way that gave one a queer, empty spot in the stomach. Now he was launched upon a story.

"This thing happened," he went on, "years ago at Roma beside the Río Bravo. I was at home alone; my wife and children were visiting in another town. I remember it was a windy night in November. The evening was cool, and, not knowing what else to do, I decided to go to bed early. I was not asleep yet when someone began pounding at my door.

"'Open the door, Don Antonio; please let me in,' said a woman's voice. I got up and recognized in the woman before me one of our new neighbors. They had just moved into a deserted *jacal* in the alley back of our house.

"'My husband is very sick,' she explained. 'He is dying and wants to see you. He says he must speak to you before he dies.'

"I dressed and went out with her, wondering all the time what this unknown man wanted to see me about. I found him in a miserable hovel, on a more miserable pallet on the floor, and I could see by his sunken cheeks and the fire that burned in his eyes that he was really dying, and of consumption, too. With mumbled words he dismissed the woman from the room and, once she had gone, he asked me to help him sit up. I propped him on the pillows the best I could. He was seized with a fit of coughing followed by a hemorrhage and I was almost sure that he would die before he could say anything. I brought him some water and poured a little *tequila* from a half empty bottle that was at the head of the pallet. After drinking it, he gave a sigh of relief.

"'I am much better now,' he whispered. His voice was already failing. 'My friend,' he went on, 'excuse my calling you, an utter stranger, but I have heard you are a man of courage and of honor and you will understand what I have to say to you. That woman you saw here is really not my wife; but I have lived with her in sin for the last twenty years. It weighs upon my conscience and I want to right the wrong I did her once.'

"As the man ended this confession, I could not help thinking what changes are brought about in the soul by the mere thought of facing eternity. I thought it very strange that after so long a time he should have qualms of conscience now. Yet I imagine death is a fearful thing, and, never having died myself nor been afraid to die, I could not judge what the dying man before me was feeling. So I decided to do what I would have expected others to do for me, and asked him if there was anything I might do for him.

"'Call a priest. I want to marry her,' he whispered.

"I did as he commanded me and went to the rectory. Father José María was still saying his prayers, and when I told him that I had come to get him to marry a dying man, he looked at me in a way he had of doing whenever he doubted anyone, with one eye half closed and out of the corner of the other. As I had played him many pranks in the past, no doubt he thought I was now playing another. He hesitated at first but then got up somewhat convinced.

"'I'll take my chance with you again, you son of Barabbas,' he said. 'I'll go. Some poor soul may want to reconcile himself with his Creator.' He put on his black cape and took the little bag he always carried on such occasions. The night was as black as the mouth of a wolf and the wind was getting colder and stronger.

"'A bad time for anyone to want a priest, eh, Father?' I said in an effort to make conversation, not knowing what else to say.

"'The hour of repentance is a blessed moment at whatever time it comes,' he replied in a tone that I thought was reprimanding.

"On entering the house, we found the man alone. The woman was in the kitchen, he told us. I joined her there, and what do you suppose the shameless creature was doing? Drinking *tequila,* getting courage, she told me, for the ordeal ahead of her. After about an hour, we were called into the sick room. The man looked much better. Unburdening his soul had given him that peaceful look you sometimes see in the face of the dead who die while smiling. I was told that I was to be witness to the Holy Sacrament of Matrimony. The woman was so drunk by now that she could hardly stand up; and between hiccoughs she promised to honor and love the man who was more fit to be food for worms than for life in this valley of tears. I'd never seen a man so strong for receiving sacraments as that one was. He had received the Sacrament of Penance, then that of Matrimony—and I could see no greater penance than marrying such a woman—and now he was to receive Extreme Unction, the Sacrament for the Dying.

"The drunken woman and I held candles as Father José María anointed him with holy oil; and when we had to join him in prayer, I was ashamed that I could not repeat even the Lord's Prayer with him. That scene will always live in my mind, and when I die may I have as holy a man as Father José María to pray for me! He lingered a few moments; then, seeing there was nothing else to do, he said he would go back. I went with him under the pretext of getting something or other for the dying man, but in reality, I wanted to see him safe at home. On the way back to the dying man I stopped at the saloon for another bottle of *tequila*. The dying man might need a few drops to give him courage to start on his journey to the Unknown, although from what I had seen I judged that Father José María had given him all he needed.

"When I returned, the death agony was upon him. The drunken woman was snoring in the kitchen. It was my responsibility to see that the man did not die like a dog. I wet his cracked lips with a piece of cloth moistured in tequila. I watched all night. The howling of the wind and the death rattle of the consumptive made the place the devil's kingdom. With the coming of dawn, the man's soul, now pure from sin, left the miserable carcass that had given it lodging during life. I folded his arms over his chest and covered his face with a cloth. There was no use in calling the woman; she lay on the dirt floor of the kitchen snoring like a trumpet. I closed the door and went to see what could be done about arrangements for the funeral. I went home and got a little money—I did not have much—to buy some boards for the coffin, black calico for the covering and for a mourning dress for the bride, now a widow—although I felt she did not deserve it—and candles.

I made the coffin, and when all was done and finished went back to the house. The woman was still snoring, her half-opened mouth filled with buzzing flies. The corpse was as I had left it. I called some of the neighbors to help me dress the dead man in my one black suit, but he was stiff already and we had to lay him in the coffin as he was, unwashed and dirty. If it is true that we wear white raiments in Heaven, I hope the good San Pedro gave him one at the entrance before the other blessed spirits got to see the pitiful things he wore. I watched the body all day; he was to be buried early the following morning. Father José María had told me he would say Mass for him. The old woman, curse her, had gotten hold of the other bottle of *tequila* and continued bottling up courage for the ordeal that she said she had to go through.

"The wind that had started the night before did not let down, in fact, it was getting stronger. Several times the candles had blown out, and the corpse and I had been left in utter darkness. To avoid the repetition of such a thing, I went to the kitchen and got some empty fruit cans very much prized by the old woman. In truth she did not want to let me use them at first, because, she said, the food on the paper wrapping looked so natural and was the only fruit she had ever owned. I got them anyway, filled them with corn, and stuck the candles there.

"Early in the evening about nine, or thereabouts, I decided to get out again and ask some people to come and watch with me part of the night. Not that I was afraid of staying alone with the corpse. One might fear the spirits of those who die in sin, but certainly not this one who had left the world the way a Christian should leave it. I left somewhat regretfully, for I was beginning to have a kindly feeling towards the dead man. I felt towards that body as I would feel towards a friend, no doubt because I had helped it to transform itself from a human being to a nice Christian corpse.

"As I went from house to house asking people to watch with me that night, I was reminded of a story that the priest had told us once, and by the time I had gone half through the town I knew very well how the man who was inviting guests to the wedding feast must have felt. All had some good excuse to give but no one could come. To make a long story short, I returned alone, to spend the last watch with my friend the corpse.

"As I neared the house, I saw it very well lightened, and I thought perhaps some people had finally taken pity upon the poor unfortunate and had gone there with more candles to light the place. But soon I realized what was really happening. The *jacal* was on fire.

"I ran inside. The sight that met my eyes was one I shall ever see. I was nailed to the floor with terror. The corpse, its hair a flamming mass, was sitting up in the coffin where it had so peacefully lain all day. Its glassy, opaque eyes stared into space with a look that saw nothing and its mouth was convulsed into the most horrible grin. I stood their paralyzed by the horror of the scene. To make matters worse the drunken woman reeled into the room, yelling, 'He is burning before he gets to Hell!'

"Two thoughts ran simultaneously through my mind: to get her out of the room and to extinguish the fire. I pushed the screaming woman out into the darkness and, arming myself with courage, reentered the room. I was wearing cowboy boots and my feet were the only part of my body well protected. Closing my eyes, I kicked the table, and I heard the thud of the burning body as it hit the floor. I became crazy then. With my booted feet I tramped upon and kicked the corpse until I thought the fire was extinguished. I dared not open my eyes for fear of what I might see, and with my eyes still closed I ran out of the house I did not stop until I reached the rectory. Like mad, I pounded upon the door, and when the priest opened it and saw me standing there looking more like a ghost than a living person, he could but cross himself. It was only after I had taken a drink or two—may God forgive me for having done so in his presence—that I could tell him what had happened.

"He went back with me and, with eyes still closed, I helped him place the poor dead man in his coffin. Father José María prayed all night. As for me, I sat staring at the wall, not daring once to look at the coffin, much less upon the charred corpse. That was the longest watch I ever kept.

"At five o'clock, with no one to help us, we carried the coffin to the church, where the promised mass was said. We hired a burro cart to take the dead man to the cemetery, and, as the sun was coming up, Father José María, that man of God, and I, an unpenitent sinner, laid him in his final resting place."

The Philosopher of the Brush Country

Tío Pancho was a distant relative of my grandfather. In fact, both bore the same given name and surname.

"We are the same Francisco," he would often say, "except that you a Don, while I in my poverty resemble the blessed Jesus. 'Poverty is loved by God,' is the saying," he would continue, "and even though a sinner, We both love the same thing." By We, he referred to God and himself. But, in spite of his supposed similarity to the Almighty, he was called *Tío Pancho Malo*. After the fashion of the simple folk among whom he lived, the surname originated not from the fact that he was bad, but from the fact that he was different. No, he was not bad. He merely had his own ideas, which he followed in his own peculiar way. And nonconformity with the general tendencies and general customs is sufficient to make anyone an outlaw amid any group of simple folk.

Tío Pancho was a philosopher, and like all philosophers, he was at outs with the world. As a young man he had lived near Mier, in Mexico, on his few ancestral acres of worthless, alkaline land. "Bitter mesquites and poor folks' children are plentiful," is

---

This story was published under the general title "Among My People," *Mary Immaculate* XVIII, 9 (1935): 262-265. This is a similar but longer version of the story published in "Among My People," in *Tone the Bell Easy,* ed. J. Frank Dobie (Austin: Texas Folk-Lore Society, 1932) 104-108, and has been reprinted in this collection of short stories by Jovita González under the title "Tío Pancho Malo." A very similar version of this story is entitled "The Philosopher of Chaparral Country" and its original manuscript is in the *E. E. Mireles & Jovita González de Mireles Papers, Special Collections & Archives, Texas A&M University-Corpus Christi Bell Library. Copyright © Texas A&M University-Corpus Christi.* All rights reserved.

an old border saying. And Tío Pancho's flock was more plentiful than the mesquite beans. His brood of boys had never had to worry about keeping clean, for during the first two years of their life they were miniature Adams, without the fig leaf—in a place far from being a Garden of Eden. When Don Francisco rebuked him because of this indecency he permitted, he would reply in his drawling voice, "Why should I interfere with the plans of my Creator? If he wanted children to wear clothes, He, in His goodness would provide them."

When his wife died, she was buried without a coffin. "Who am I," he explained, "that I should prevent Nature from fulfilling her end? The sooner she mingles with Mother Nature the sooner her destiny is fulfilled." After her death he and his boys moved to Texas, where he became a *pastor,* not of souls, but of goats. When the flock did not demand too much attention, he planted a few acres of land. One day the people at grandfather's ranch were driven to hysterics by the appearance of the boys wearing gourds for hats.

"What is the object of a hat?" he asked. "Is it not protection from the elements? There in the shape of a gourd Nature has provided us with something that serves the same purpose and that does not cost anything." He could neither read nor write; yet he composed poetry and expressed himself in a most flowery language. One day when he wanted an ax he commanded one of his sons to bring him "that bright shiny object which man in his cruelty uses for the decapitation of defenseless trees." On another occasion, as he was returning from his native Mier to Texas he was stopped by the customs officers, and on being asked what he had in a bag he carried replied:

"Sir, they are manufactures of wheat, with incrustations of *piloncillo* (brown sugar) which in your country are called coffee cakes, but in mine, plain sweet bread." On being told that he could go, his reply was equally verbose;

"Thanks good sir, you are an ocean of kindness wherein navigates the bark of gratitude."

When the boys grew up, his great exploit was the organization of a band. He did not know any music; neither did his sons. But what difference did that make to Pancho? Their instruments were of the most rudimentary types; reed flutes, handmade guitars, an old fife, a trombone, cymbals and a drum. As director, Tío Pancho Malo led this band from ranch to ranch, playing and improvising as the spirit moved them. One day they came to Grandfather's ranch and a more raggedy bunch was never seen. They played a few selections and Don Francisco asked the director if they played by note.

"No," Tío Pancho Malo replied, "we are not injust in our demands; we play for chickens, beans, corn or whatever the rancheros may have, but we never require a note."

He was very proud of his sons' accomplishments as musicians, and often paid them compliments but never in their presence.

"My Tirso," he confided to Don Francisco, "plays the trombone with the strength of an ox."

The World War found Tío Pancho Malo with six husky, strapping boys, all physically fit and of age for service. However, he did not want them to serve in the army. "Why should they fight," he argued, "for a country that is not ours? First the *Americanos* get this land from us, but that might have been our fault though; we could not defend it like men and now we weep for it like women. However, why should our sons fight merely because a King was killed in a country far from us? Why should we worry when we have enough troubles at home; the drought, the sand storms, and the need of grass for the goats and sheep? Besides, why should they fight some poor Christians who have done us no harm? No, my sons will not be in the army." And to prevent this, he and his sons started trekking back to the old town of Mier.

The peaceful muddy Bravo, like a thread of quicksilver, was already visible, and the party was within an hour from safety when the Rangers came upon them.

"You keep your mouth shut," said Tío Pancho Malo to his sons, "I shall talk to them and convice them that I am right." On being asked where they were going and why, Tío Pancho answered in the high flown way that characterized him:

"Most esteemable gentleman, you inquire of me my destination and why I am traveling in this direction. Your ears shall be regaled by my narrative. Most worthy gentlemen," he continued with a bow, "I am taking these, my sons, to the birthplace of their ancestors, Mier, the heroic city that defeated at one time a band of Americans. No offense intended, *señores;* I am taking them there because I do not want them to fight, for your goverment. My sons are not cowards; they can, and will fight, but only when they have received an offense. How can they fight against people who have never wronged them and who they have never seen? We are sorry for the King that was killed and if you think it fitting and proper we can even write a letter of condolence to his widow, but as to fighting, that is another matter. I prefer my sons should not get involved in a fight that is not theirs."

"Do you know who you are talking to?"asked one of the Rangers.

"Most esteemable *señor,* yes sir; you are a Ranger."

"Don't you know I have the power to arrest you and your sons also?"

"Most certainly, we know that."

"Then why have you not tried to evade my questions?"

"My father, may he be in a choir of Angels now, did not teach me to lie, *señor.*"

Only the youngest remained with him; the others were drafted and after the necessary training went to fight their unknown foes, never to return. The youngest died of small pox. Tío Pancho was left alone, and he went up and down the river from ranch to ranch expounding his theories and his queer philosophy.

He would not touch one cent of the insurance due him. "This money is the price of innocent blood spilled in a useless war. If I accepted it I would feel like the butcher of my boys," he contended.

As time went on he was seen no more in the border ranches. Years passed and no one knew what had become of him. My grandfather often wondered and so did grandmother; they had inquired repeatedly on their trips to town, but with no results. Then one day when they were least expecting it, Tío Esteban, the mail carrier, brought a letter signed by the sheriff of a county to the north. In it, Don Francisco was informed that his namesake was in jail for some petty offense; and, continued the letter, the accused would like to have his relative come to his aid.

Grandfather left immediately, and two days later he arrived at the county seat. Not even wanting to change his travel-stained clothes, he went to the jail were Tío Pancho was detained.

Don Francisco found his namesake, in a pitiful condition, ragged and dirty but smoking a cigarette and very much at ease. His eyes were as bright as ever, and the tongue remained ever as sharp.

"Just look how low the name of Olivares has sunk, Francisco," Tío Pancho told his cousin, "to be in jail is not so much of a disgrace, for jail was made for men, but to be placed here by women, *ay!* that's the galling part. Those long-nosed, hatched-faced, inquisitive daughters of Satan have placed me here."

"But why? What have you done?"

"That's what I ignore, my cousin. I was peacefully carrying a barrel of water one day, when a group of these so-called ladies stopped me. At first I thought they wanted a barrel of water as my chest expanded with pride, as much as my old ribs could, to see that these American ladies needed my poor services.

"We are in luck today, Lycurgus!" I told my donkey; "this is were we make a dime, two big fat nickles; now you can have all the hay you can eat." I asked the ladies in what my poor humble person could serve them.

"They asked my name, where I lived, looked Lycurgus all over very carefully, poked his ribs, looked into his mouth, and then I told them that my Lycurgus was not for sale because to part with him was to part with half of my life. "If you take him, my dear ladies, you will have to take me," I said to them. I specialy addressed one who seemed more interested than the rest. She was thinner than my Lycurgus, and I bet if I poked her as she did my donkey, I would have been able to count every bone in her body; as to teeth I suppose Lycurgus had more. As I said before, I specially adressed her, for I could see that she was the leader of the group, and when I said, "you will have to take me," I really believe the old one thought I was offering myself in marriage, for she gave a mouse-like squeal and ran off. Then they all left, and I remained alone, thinking to myself how strange it all was.

"The next day I was arrested and brought here—I am not worried about myself, but I am about my poor Lycurgus; where can he be? He who would not eat unless I fed him with my own hands and would not sleep unless I slapped him good-night. Will you find him for me? That's what I called you for."

"You sent for me so I could look for your donkey?"

"Yes, Francisco; I am a man and I can look after myself but my poor Lycurgus, he is such a timid, bashful donkey. I am afraid for him."

Strange indeed were the ways of men, mused Don Francisco as he went to look for the lost donkey. He did not look long. He found Lycurgus still harnessed to the water cart, patiently waiting for his master to come. After Tío Pancho's arrest the poor creature's instinct told him to go home, and he waited four days and four nights at the gate of his master's shack.

Don Francisco had his servant unharness the poor beast, and had him taken to the stable where his own horse was kept.

"Now that I have looked after the donkey I must see about yourself," Don Francisco told Tío Pancho; "you must have some clothes in which to appear, and I shall look around for someone to defend you."

"To defend me? Ah, Francisco, who can be the best lawyer for the accused, than the accused himself. I shall defend myself and don't you worry about me, I shall know best what to say. As to clothes, I shall permit you to bring them not for my sake, but for yours; I would not want you to be ashamed of me."

The day for the trial came, and still Tío Pancho did not know what he was charged with; neither had he allowed Don Francisco to find out.

The court room was filled; Tío Pancho was well known, and many had come out of curiosity to hear what the old man would say.

He was brought in by a deputy sheriff. His new suit, new shoes, and recent haircut and shave made him feel and act a little unnatural at first. He looked at Don Francisco and raised his hand in salutation. He then looked around the room, smiled at all his friends, until his eyes rested on the ladies that had been the cause of his downfall. He stopped in the middle of the room, bowed and adressed them:

"*Buenos días, señoras,* he who is suffering the injustice of mankind salutes you." With that he sat down.

"Francisco de los Olivares, accused of cruelty to his donkey," called out the judge.

So that was it! They were accusing him of being cruel to Lycurgus, he who fed him, and cared for him, while they, the ladies with the flowered hats, had left him harnessed to wander through the streets hungry and tired as he was.

One after another the ladies testified against him. In harrowing words they all told the story of how poor and thin Lycurgus was, how pathethic and hungry he looked.

When asked if he had anything to say to his accusation he stood erect and looking straight at the accusers replied:

"Your Honor," he told the judge, "these good ladies have accused me of cruelty towards my donkey, saying that I make the poor skinny creature work. But these good ladies have not stopped to consider that I am also poor, skinny and have to work. The donkey and I live for each other. Without me he would starve; without him I would die of hunger. We work together and for each other. If these ladies prevent his working, both of us will starve, and that in my mind would be not only cruelty to animals but cruelty to me."

The court could do nothing but let Tío Pancho Malo go.

Don Francisco wanted to take him along with him to the Olivareño but the old fellow would not go.

"Spare me the disgrace of being an object of charity," he told his relative; I have always worked for myself, and I want to continue doing so until I go to join my family. Lycurgus and I will work for each other. We both love poverty as I have often told you, and I am happy. *Adiós,* Francisco."

A short time later he died, leaving his savings for the care of donkeys which, like his, had been the friends of man.

Among My People. Border Folklore

It was August down in the Rio Grande. The rays of the sun beat mercilessly upon the sandy stretches of grass-covered prairie which glared angrily back at the sun. Gleamingly white, under the scorching sun, on a bend of *el camino real,* the king's highway, stood a pretentious house, rambling and flat roofed. Its grilled doors and windows and thick adobe walls showed its Spanish or Mexican descendency. Stone benches, called, *pollitos,* because they were attached and formed part of the house, were on either side of the main door. Hackberry and cotton wood trees shaded the *patio* on the west side and a few pomegranate trees and oleanders in bloom added color to the landscape. A maguey fence surrounded the house, and the iron grilled gate swung from an ebony tree post, and was latched to another by a handmade lock.

A man riding a spirited horse rode to the gate and descending with a leap tied his mount to the salt cedar by the gate. He was tall and slender, and in spite of his gray hair had the agility of youth. His lean face with its pointed beard was striking because of its clear cut features, and deep set gray eyes. His tight fitting brown suit, black sash and gay *sarape* over one shoulder showed to advantage the slender body of a man who although

This story was published as a part of a group of stories under the general title "Among My People" in the magazine *Mary Immaculate* XVIII, 6 (1935) 172-175. This story is also a part of Chapter II "The Stronghold of the Olivares" of the novel *Dew on the Thorn* by Jovita González (Houston: Arte Público Press, 1997) 12-31. The version of the story published in this collection belongs to the one presented in the *Mary Immaculate* magazine.

past his sixtieth year was still in the prime of manhood. He walked with arrogance, his silver spurs clinking on the brick floor of the *patio* as he rolled a long cigarette.

He stopped as though struck by a sudden thought. He looked to the north, to the south, and to the east. Beyond, for miles lay the pastures for his herds of cattle and his flocks of sheep. He gave a sigh of satisfaction and murmured softly to himself:

"Our land, the land of our fathers, and the land of our children." The sun, a ball of orange pink was descending down the horizon at one stride, and a soft cooling breeze, the pulmotor of the borderland sprung from the east. Down in the *cañada* (canebrake), which ran by the ranch the doves were cooing and the redbirds in the cotton wood grove by the dirt "tank" near the house began to sing. From the corrals came the voice of the *vaqueros* singing and jesting, and blended with bleating of the goats and the sheep were the whistles and hisses of the *pastor.* The shrill garrulous stridulations of the locusts completed the chorus of the evening noises. Darkness subdued them, then as the moon came up an unaccounted mob of mongrel curs set up a barking at it that the coyotes out beyond reach mocked.

As he stood there, the beauty and pastoral simplicity of the scene brought to his mind thoughts of the past. He saw himself, a child of twelve, at the bedside of a dying man; his mother kneeling at the foot of the bed, saying *De Profundis,* the prayer for the dying, and the priest blessing the sick man. He could hear his gasping words, "Francisco, my son, soon you will be head of the family, be the protector of your mother, and the guardian of your sister. Remember yours is an honorable name and above all never forget the heroic deeds of your people. In time of trouble, in time of stress, let the motto of our family be your guide, 'Like an oak I may get bent but not broke.' "My son," the dying man continued, "when you become a man take the cattle across the Bravo into Texas the land which the viceroy deeded my grandfa-

ther, Don José Alejandro, it is our heritage which I leave to you.
And may God and His holy Mother be your guide."

D on Cesareo was buried under the altar of the church as was
due one of his rank, and Doña Ramona, his widow became
the mistress of his possessions. She had a will of iron, ruled the
peones with an iron hand and had the respect of all. He could see
her, contrary to the custom of her time, riding with him and the
vaqueros to the pastures whenever necessity required it of her.
He remembered how once, her small, slender frame shaking with
anger and indignation she had slapped a *vaquero* who had dared
to use an ugly word in her presence.

He remembered her as the head of the household, stern and
severe, her pale face, clear cut as an ivory cameo, contrasting
with the snappy black eyes that saw everything and shone like
burning coals when provoked to anger. And again her memory
came to him, but in different mood; not as the mistress to be
feared, but as the mother taking her children to church. Dressed
in black, a mother of pearl and silver crucifix on her breast, lace
mantilla covering the soft wavy hair, just turning gray, she was
like a mourning madonna, a *Mater Dolorosa,* ever anxious for
her children.

Grown to early manhood he remembered making love to the
servant girls with the ardor and impetuousness of youth. He saw
himself facing Doña Ramona in her room, her hair almost white
now, framed her deep lined face. But her eyes had retained the fire
and spirit of former times. Unable to stand the look of disgust and
contempt in them he had stooped to kiss her hand, but she had
jerked it away with violence. "The kiss of one who is not a gentleman soils my hand," he heard her say. Another scene came to
his mind; it was his wedding day. Contrary to tradition and his
mother's wishes he was not wearing the black formal suit. He was

a *ranchero* and he preferred to dress like one. The finest buckskin suit trimmed in silver buttons had been brought from Saltillo for the occasion. Again he stood in his mother's room but this time for a mother's blessing. "Francisco, my first born," she said "dearer to me than life itself, tomorrow you will leave me to fulfill your father's wish. My heart bleeds for you when I see you go to another land. You will enter into the heritage of your ancestors, but you will be ruled by people who are the born enemies of your race. But remember my boy, wherever you may be, wherever you may go you are the heir of a proud name, and a prouder race. Keep your faith and be what you were destined to be, a Mexican and a gentleman."

The scene changed again:

He could hear the cowboys urging and encouraging the frightened cattle to cross the river—he saw an ox cart loaded with household goods awaiting on the northern side of the stream—a young girl, silent tears rolling down her cheeks, stood by his side waving good-bye to those across the river.

Trembling with joy and emotion he found himself again in his mother's presence, a newborn baby in his arms.

"He is your *mi madre,* hold him in your arms and bless him."

"Your first son and born in God's land."

"Of course my mother, did you ever think I'd want him to bear the traitor's brand? I've already registered him in the Palacio, Francisco José Alejandro, a proud name. No child of mine will ever be in Texas."

He had worked hard, and the heritage of his father was now one of the richest ranches in the lower Rio Grande. He had more cattle, more horses, more mules, more sheep, and more goats than any other *ranchero.* In his spacious house, he lived like a feudal lord; ever in readiness to receive friends and foes, the former with open arms, the latter with ready arms. As head of his family, he led a patriarchal existence, his word was authority, no other law was needed and there was no need of civil interference.

He was master of everything not only the land he possessed but of the *peones* who worked the soil.

❧ ❧ ❧

A tyrant by temperament, Don Francisco was feared and respected by all who knew him. If he appeared in the corral riding his powerful black horse, his eyes contracted in a frown, one higher than the other; the stoutest *vaquero* trembled in his boots. Don Francisco's expression was the sign of a tempest that would soon hurl itself with the fury of a tropical tornado. As he rode through his possessions lashing the *vaqueros* with his tongue and not seldom with his *riata* no one dared utter a word.

And Don Francisco had kept his word. Every time a son or daughter was expected the family crossed the Rio Grande to the land of his fathers to await the arrival of the little stranger. Proud, aristocratic and a gentleman by inheritance he had retained those characteristics in the wilderness in which he lived. He was proud of two things, that he was a Mexican, and that the land he possessed had been in the family for generations past. His one endeavor was to make his ranch a miniature Mexico. His family was encouraged and expected to keep intact the customs and traditions of the mother country; the servants and *peones* were commanded to follow in the footsteps of their brethren in Mexico.

But though he was a master of many he was the slave of one—Doña Margarita, his wife. And as he thundered through the rooms of his spacious house, his spurs echoing through the cement floors, one look from his wife was sufficient to calm him.

"Francisco, my lamb, let me read to you a while." Then the lion now a lamb indeed, would sit by her while she read to him from the lives of the saints, *Romeo and Juliet,* or some romantic novel. She played the organ and the accordion, and when her reading was not sufficient to soothe Don Francisco, she played melodies that both had loved in their youth. Doña Margarita was the undisputed mistress of her home, her eight children, and the women of the ranch. Every evening the ranch people gathered in the *sala* to hear music from the phonograph, or stories from Doña Margarita. The gatherings always ended with prayers, led by the mistress of the house and always puntuated by commands or reproofs.

"Hail Mary full of grace—Francisco, you are nodding my love, The Lord is with thee—Felipe, stop tickling your sister, Blessed art thou amongst women—Francisco, I heard you snore." And so it went.

Among My People

In spite of his twelve years there was something about José María that made him act old. A certain sadness, a certain indescribable melancholy permeated a spirit which should have been that of a child. His long, thin face, pale and sad, had the ascetic beauty of a Mediaeval saint, and his black, haunting eyes had neither the light nor the sparkle of youth. He spoke in monosyllables, never laughed, and his smile, when he smiled, was bitter. It was the smile of a soul that weeps. He was a tragic figure on horseback as he rode by seeking the loneliness of the pastures.

A group of women doing their weekly laundry at the creek stopped their work as they saw him approach.

"He is bewitched," said the oldest of the group.

"And possessed of an evil spirit besides," asserted another.

"They say he talks to the dead," added a young girl who with water jar on head had just arrived.

"Yes, and at night he and three devils play ball with the eyes of sleepy children who have been naughty during the day," said a young mother pinching her seven-year-old boy in a warning manner.

This story was published under the general title: "Among My People," *Mary Immacuate* XVIII, 8 (1935) 230-232. This story is also part of Chapter III "Border Honor" of the novel *Dew On The Thorn* (Houston: Arte Público Press, 1997) 32-44 by Jovita González and edited by José E. Limón. Although in both stories the names of some characters and places have been changed, the plot of the story remains the same.

Unconscious of all the comments he was creating the boy passed the woman, and with the innate grace of his forbears greeted them.

"What a pity," sighed the girl, "he is such a handsome little fellow."

"If I was his father I would whip the devil out of him."

"Whip the devil out of him?" queried Clementina, "how can that be done?"

"Easy enough. The same as his father whipped the devil out of Doña Rita."

"How strange! I had never heard of that before. Tell me about it," begged the girl putting her jar down.

"It was this way," began the old grandmother ever ready to tell a story, as she rolled her corn shuck cigarette.

"You town people are ignorant of many things. You may believe me and then you may not, just as you please. When José María was little, just the age of Manuelito here, his mother took sick. It was a strange malady, she turned yellow and would neither sleep, talk nor eat. She just laid in bed and stared at the ceiling of the room. None of us could see what she saw there. Don Ramón, her husband, who knows something about healing thought at first it was her heart. He gave her *torongil* tea with powdered deer blood to drink for nine consecutive mornings, but that did not cure her malady. He then gave her *cenizo* tea, which if left outdoors to be cooled by the dew will cure any liver trouble. But that did not make her feel better. The poor man not knowing what to do came to me for advice. I knew full well that Doña Rita was bewitched, but those things are better left unsaid so I suggested that he go with Tío Anselmo, the witch healer. Well, he went," continued the old woman blowing rings of smoke as she spoke. "Tío Anselmo was no fool and he knew right away what to do. He told Don Ramón to go to the creek and gather all the chili peppers he could find, and to make a fire with them, close all the doors and windows, and place Doña Rita by the open fireplace. The suffocating vapors would either choke or drive the evil spirits away. This done he was to whip her with a raw hide rope, folded three times. Tío Anselmo told Don Ramón not to mind Rita's screams at all. He would not hurt her but the evil spirits that possessed her.

"In the meantime, José María, unseen by anyone, had come into the room and hidden by the darkness was watching, his little white face streaked with tears as he saw his mother writhe in agony under the merciless blows of his father. Her screams ceased and she fell in a faint. For months she was more dead than alive. I think she would have died too, had it not been for the youngest of her seven children, José María, who with pale sorrowful face of the Crucified sat by her bedside day and night and looked with eyes that saw nothing.

"She recovered, but, and this is the thing that we dare not to say," the grandmother finished in confidental whisper, "it is thought that the evil spirit that left the mother took possession of the boy, for since then he goes about silent, looking at the world with the hauting eyes of the possessed."

So engrossed were the women in the story that they did not hear the approaching hoofs of a rider.

"Good morning, *amigas,*" he cried to the women as he dismounted with the quickness of an expert rider.

"Don Ramón," whispered old Juana, "may the Lord have mercy upon our souls if he suspects we have been talking about him."

The women answered his salutation and went back to their forgotten washing.

On this particular day he seemed to be in a hurry. While his horse drank at the stream he paced up and down under the shade of a gigantic mesquite tree. He gave a shrill whistle which was soon answered by the arrival of a boy; it was José María.

"Tell your mother," he said, "not to expect me early, I am going to my *compadre* Francisco's ranch and will not be home until dark."

In a few minutes he covered the distance that separated him from his friend's ranch. Don Ramón found him sitting in the patio smoking his after *siesta* cigarette. In true Mexican fashion they embraced each other warmly and slapped each other on the shoulder with the vehemence of their race.

"*Bien, compadre,* sit down and tell me what you know. Where is that rascal Juanillo? He was here a moment ago. Here, you good for nothing Indian, bring Don Ramón a chair. You simply cannot treat *peones* like human beings," he said turning to his friend, "as soon as you do they think themselves better than their masters. Away with you," he said to the returning boy, "go feed my horse, and see that you do it better than you did the last time. Now sit down, *amigo.*"

They talked of trival things, the *remuda,* the approaching visit of the missionary priest, the love affairs of the servants. One thing led to another until the conversation came to the thing nearest Don Ramón's heart, his oldest son, Carlos.

"He is a very devil, that boy is, a very Don Juan; why *compadre*" he boosted proudly, "he can outdance and outdrink any young *caballero* in the community, and as to love affairs, all I can say is that I envy him."

"At your age, *compadre!*"

"Bah! you talk like an old woman."

"Like a gentleman, my friend."

"Where love affairs are concerned who is one at Carlos' age? He is young, and youth, like birds need wings. I often tell him, 'My boy, youth is a divine treasure that leaves us never to return, make the best of it, but never forget the honor of a man, and above all, keep your name which is mine above reproach.'"

"Right you are, Ramón, but remember one thing, youth, health, and money cannot be wasted ruthlessly."

"Pooh, pooh, again you talk like an old woman. Carlos will settle down and be a family man like all of us."

"And what nice girl will have him?

"Any one; the more love affairs he has, the more acceptable he will be. A man has to have his affairs to be a man, and besides isn't woman the depository of family honor? Rosita will see to that when they marry. Do you know what the rascal is doing now?" he added not noticing the frown of disgust on his friend's face, "making love to that pretty Carmela, old Juana's grandaughter. She came to me, the old woman did to complain of Carlos' behavior towards the girl, 'Coop up your little chicken for my little rooster has the world to roam!' I told her. What are we coming to? In my day the daughter of a *peón* considered herself honored if the young master noticed her."

"For shame, *compadre,* how can you talk that way? How disgusting it would be to see in low born creatures the likeness of your ancestors."

"Perhaps you are right, my friend, but I did not come to speak to you about my boy, came to consult you about more serious things."

"More serious than Carlos' affairs?"

"Pshaw, *compadre,* the love affairs of youth are like the rosy clouds of dawn. They disappear with time."

"I shall make my daughter see it that way, and as for Carlos—"

"He will settle down when he marries Rosita and will be a better husband for his experiences."

The call to the *merienda* put an end to the conversation.

It was four o'clock by the kitchen clock and the shadow which the sun dial projected. The meal was served under the *portal* used as dining room in the summer. A long homemade table covered with a red and white tablecloth was loaded with ranch delicacies; flour *tortillas,* pastry rich with powdered sugar and cinnamon, fresh corn muffins, cheese made that morning, pumpkin pies and newly roasted coffee with the fragant flavor of the tropics. The conversation now became more general and pleasant with the addition of the ladies of the house. The meal ended, the women left the table, and the two men resumed their conversation.

"What I really came to see you about," said Don Francisco, "is to get your opinion about the stealing of cattle that's been worrying everyone. How many have you lost?"

"Fifty of the fattest and best of the herd."

"I have not lost that many, twenty at the most, the heaviest losers I understand are the people at Casa Verde ranch. They are *gringos* though it really does not matter."

"Why do you say that, are they not good neighbors?"

"Yes, a thousand devils take them, but the *gringo* I like is a dead *gringo.* Some day I am going to move to the city and buy a home near the American cemetery."

"What a strange desire!"

"Oh, it will be great, *compadre!* As far as the eye can see I will see thousands of graves, and just think in every one will be a dead *gringo.* All dead, compadre."

"No one but you would think of that at this time," laughed Don Francisco.

"What I think," continued Don Ramón getting serious again, "is this; but this I say to you alone. The cattle thieves are people whom we know, who know us and know in what pastures we keep the best cattle."

"Impossible! What you say is absurd. Does that then mean that it might be you or me?"

"Exactly."

"Do you realize that you are accusing the whole community?"

"Yes, I do, but I also realize that the only way of finding the thieves is to arouse the *rancheros* to action."

"I see the *caporal* hurriedly coming this way; he may have something to say. Well, what is it?" asked the *ranchero* as José entered, "have we lost more cattle?"

"No, *señor,* but Las Casas Blancas ranch was robbed last night, the thieves got away with five hundred dollars from the ranch store and the post office."

"That's an outrage, and we stand here and allow this to happen?"

"Notify the rangers, *señor.*"

"How like one of your caste you talk," blurted out Don Ramón, "keep this in your slow moving mind; we the Mexicans of the Texas ranches have never needed the rangers, and never shall. The rangers are not for men who are men. We can fight our own fights without the need of their interference. Do you understand that?"

"Yes, señor."

"If the cattle thieves are *gringos* as they can very well be we can deal with them, if they are of 'ours' we can handle them, too. It has been done before and it can be done again."

"What would be the best way to proceed?" asked Don Ramón.

"The priest is coming Sunday, and all the ranchmen will be here over the services. Suppose we discuss it then. We shall teach this thieving vermin a lesson that they will never forget."

"*Muy bien,* very well, until Sunday then, *compadre.*"

"If God wills it. *Adiós.*"

The spirited pawing of a horse was heard, followed by a swift gallop. From the distance came the echoes of a song.

"With wounded soul and mournful thought
A fading face and a wounded heart."

Don Ramón going home.

Religious Tales

El Cardo Santo (The Thistle)

One time there were two *compadres* who, although they were good friends, always contradicted each other. And this was because one, whom we shall call Juan, always saw the good and beautiful side of life, and the other, Antonio, always took pleasure in seeing the unpleasant and ugly side of things.

As the two were out in the *potrero* (pasture) one day, Juan said "Don't you think, *compadre,* that the mesquites look pretty today? The bloom is heavy and that means abundant food for the pigs this winter."

"Humph, growled Antonio, "how can you call them beautiful when the thorns are so sharp you can't touch them without killing yourself in the attempt?"

The two continued their way, Juan seeing the beauty of cactus and the *pitahaya*[†] (or *pitalla*) in bloom, smelling the fragrance of the *huisache* and the *uña de gato* (catsclaw), while Antonio saw only the thorns and wastefulness of Nature in creating things that a person could not pluck and gather at his will.

"And the priest says that God knows what he does. The idea of plants having thorns!" he grumbled.

Jovita González, "Folk-Lore of the Texan-Mexican *Vaquero*," *Texas and Southwestern Lore,* ed. J. Frank Dobie (Austin: Folk-Lore Society, 1927) 12-13

[†]A cactus growing on the dry rocky soil of the border land. It bears a purple-red flower and a palatable fruit similar in the taste to the strawberry. The soldiers of Fort Rinngold, Rio Grande, call it Mexican strawberry. The cactus itself is used to make candy. There is a candy shop on Alamo Plaza, San Antonio, where *pitalla* candy is made.

"Hush, *compadre*," replied Juan, "the Virgin will punish you."

"What else can I expect when this world is upside down?" continued Antonio.

The rest of the day they rode in silence. At evening, having come to a *laguna,* they decided to camp for the night. Antonio found fault with everything, first with the night because it was too dark, and then when the moon came up, because the brightness kept him from going to sleep.

Finally he went to sleep. Soon he was dreaming, but even the dream displeased him, for in it he saw a great radiance, something like a cloud of light, approaching. In the midst of the cloud he saw a lady, holding an armful of lavender and pink flowers. The presence spoke to him with a voice that sounded like the singing of all the spring birds.

"Antonio," it said, "I have heard your words of displeasure and because I love the *vaqueros*, I have brought you a thorn-less flower that you can pluck, and fondle, and love."

With these words the lady disappeared, leaving Antonio stunned at what he had seen and heard. When he awoke, there, growing beside him, was a thistle-like flower, which he called *Cardo Santo,* for it was a holy gift of the Virgin.

The Guadalupana Vine

In south Texas there is a vine used for medicinal purposes known as the Guadalupana vine. It bears small gourd-like fruit. The seeds have a bright red covering, which on being removed show the image of our Lady of Guadalupe. Everybody is acquainted with the story of the apparition of our Lady of Guadalupe in Mexico. The story of the vine in itself is equally as interesting.

Two *vaqueros* were going to the nearest town for provisions. One of them was riding a very spirited *potro*. On coming to a creek the horse was frightened, and in spite of all that the rider could do the bronco threw him on the rocky banks. The other, terrified by the accident, did not know how to help his companion, who was slowly bleeding to death. As he sat there, a lovely lady came to him. She was dressed in blue, and he noticed that her mantle was sprinkled with stars. What astonished him more was to see that she floated, her feet not touching the ground. But he attributed this phenomenon to his bewildered condition. She approached, holding a small red fruit in her hand.

Jovita González, "Folk-Lore of the Texan-Mexican Vaquero," *Texas and Southwestern Lore,* ed. J. Frank Dobie (Austin: Folk-Lore Society, 1927) 13-14. This story was republished in "Stories of My People," *Texas Folk and Folklore,* eds. Mody C. Boatright, William H. Hudson and Allen Maxwell (Dallas: Southern Methodist University Press, 1954) 23-24.

"Try this, my son," the lady said; dip it in *mescal* and put it in the wound."

"But it will burn," stammered the surprised *vaquero*. The lovely lady smiled, shook her head, and whispered, "*No arde, no arde.*" ("It will not burn.")

The *vaquero* did as he was told, and, strange as it may seem, his companion was cured immediately. The *vaqueros* consider this a miracle of the Virgin, and to verify this story they point to the fact that the Virgin left her image engraved on all the seed.[†]

[†]On the border, the Mexican housewife puts up jars of the Guadalupe fruit in *mescal*. The people use no other remedy for cuts and wounds.

The Dove

Do you know why the dove ever mourns? This is the story so common among Mexican people.

All nature, the stars of the heavens, the beasts of the forest, and the birds of the air had been told that the Messiah was to be born. And when the Angel announced the birth of the Savior, all the creatures of the earth came to worship Him, all but one—the dove. She was so humble and unassuming that no one thought of telling her the wonderful news. Yet the sign that brought the birds and beasts to the manger itself was the form of a fluttering dove—assumed by the Holy Spirit.

But the dove herself never saw the Christ Child, and that is why her song is a sob. In the mellow warm mornings of spring, or when the evening star makes her appearance in the twilight, a soft, mournful cry is heard in the *cañada*. It is the dove.

Jovita González, "Tales and Songs of the Texas-Mexicans," *Man, Bird and Beast,* Ed. J Frank Dobie (Austin: Folk-Lore Society, 1932) 98. This story was republished in "Stories of My People," *Texas Folk and Folklore,* eds. Mody C. Boatright, William H. Hudson and Allen Maxwell (Dallas: Southern Methodist University Press, 1954) 22.

El Cenizo

It had been an unusually hard winter, cold and dry. But then coyotes had in the fall announced it would be so, for their fur had been heavy and thick, and they had stayed close to the ranches, not daring to go to the hills. All vegetation had been killed by *el hielo prieto* (the black frost), and even the cactus, the always reliable food for the cattle, had wilted.

Spring came, and with it new hope. But whatever young, green things sprang up died for need of water. The mesquites were mere ghosts; the *huisache,* shameful of not bearing their sweet-smelling velvety blooms, hid their leaves. All the waterholes had dried up, and death and starvation ruled the prairie. The buzzard was lord of the plains, and as it flew over the trees was a constant reminder of death. The cattle, once so plentiful and fat, had diminished to a few, and those that remained looked at the world with sad, death-like eyes.

"*¿Por qué no llueve, Dios mío?*" ("Why do you not make it rain, my Lord?") the *vaquero* said, looking up at the sky. And with a sigh of resignation he added, "*Así es la suerte.*" ("That's luck.")

There was just one possible way of salvation, and that was prayer, prayer to the Virgin. The cowmen gathered together and reverently knelt on the plain to beg for help. As the last prayer of

Jovita González, "Folk-Lore of the Texan-Mexican Vaquero," *Texas and Southwestern Lore,* ed. J. Frank Dobie (Austin: Folk-Lore Society, 1927) 9-10.

the rosary was said, a soft breeze, a *lagueño*[†] blew from the east. Soon drops began to fall; all night the rain fell like a benediction.

Filled with new hope, the people rose early the next day to see the blessing that had fallen over the land, and indeed it was a beautiful blessing. For as far as the eye could see, the plain was covered with silvery shrubs, sparkling with raindrops and covered with flowers, pink, lavender and white.

It was a gift from the Virgin, and because the day was Ash Wednesday the shrub was called *el cenizo*.[††] The interpretation given by the *vaquero* is charming, to say the least; the gray of the leaves signifies the Passion of Christ; the white flowers, the purity of the mother; and the pink, the new dawn for the cowmen and the resurrection of life.

[†]A breeze from the Gulf.

[††]*Ceniza* means *ashes*. The shrub is common all over Southwest Texas, and is known to country people of that section only by the Mexican name, *cenizo* or *ceniza* (pronounced *cenisa*), a name probably derived from the ashen color of the leaves. The botanical term is *Leucophyllum texanum*. Nurseries are popularizing it as shrub for landscape planting—and it certainly has a great deal more character than the ligustrum! In the more arid parts of Texas it blooms after summer rain; it is evergreen—or, more accurately, everashen. Mexicans make a medicinal tea of it.

Tales of Popular Customs

Shelling Corn by Moonlight

In August, down towards the Rio Grande, the rays of the sun beat vertically upon the sandy stretches of land, from which all tender vegetation has been scorched, and the white, naked land glares back at the sun; the only palpitating thing discoverable between the two poles of heat are heat devils. The rattlesnakes are as deeply holed up and as quiet as in mid-winter. In the thickets of brush the road-runners, rusty lizards, mockingbirds and all other living things pant. Whirlwinds dance across the stretches of prairie interspersed between the thickets of thorn. At six o'clock it is hotter than at mid-day. Seven o'clock, and then the sun, a ball of orange pink, descends below the horizon at one stride. The change is magical. A soft cooling breeze, the pulmotor of the border lands, springs up from the south.

Down in the *cañada,* which runs by the ranch, doves coo. Out beyond cattle are grazing and calves are frisking. In the cottonwood tree growing beside the dirt "tank" near the ranch house the redbird sings. Children shout and play. From the corrals come the voices of *vaqueros* singing and jesting. Blended with the bleatings of goats and sheep are the whistles and hisses of the *pastor* (shepherd). The shrill garrulous stridulations of locusts complete the chorus of evening noises. Darkness subdues them;

Jovita González, "Among My People," *Tone the Bell Easy,* ed. J. Frank Dobie(Austin:Texas Folk-Lore Society, 1932) 99-101. This story was republished in *Mexican American Authors,* eds. Américo Paredes and Raymund Paredes (Boston: Houghton-Mifflin, 1972) 8-10.

then as the moon rises, an uncounted mob of mongrel curs set up a howling and barking at it that coyotes out beyond mock.

It was on a night like this that the ranch folk gathered at the Big House to shell corn. All came: Tío Julianito, the *pastor,* with his brood of black half-starved children ever eager for food; Alejo, the fiddler; Juanito the idiot, called the Innocent, because the Lord was keeping his mind in Heaven; Pedro the hunter, who had seen the world and spoke English; the *vaqueros*; and on rare occasions, Tío Esteban, the mail carrier. Even the women came, for on such occasions supper was served.

A big canvas was spread outside in front of the kitchen. In the center of this canvas ears of corn were piled in pyramids for the shellers, who sat about in a circle and with their bare hands shelled the grains off the cobs.

It was then, under the moonlit sky, that we heard stories of witches, buried treasures, and ghosts. I remember one in particular that sent chills up and down my spine.

"'The night was dark, gloomy; the wind moaned over the tree tops, and the coyotes howled all around. A knock was heard; the only occupant limped across the room and opened the door. A blast of cold wind put out the candle.

"'Who is there?' he asked, looking out into a night as dark as the mouth of a wolf.

"'Just a lost hermit,' answered a wailing voice. 'Will you give a stranger a lodging for the night?'

"A figure wrapped in a black cape entered, and as he entered a tomb-like darkness and coldness filled the room.

"'Will you take off your hat and cape?' the host asked solicitously of his mysterious guest.

"'No—but—I shall—-take off my head.' And saying this, the strange personage placed his head, a skull, upon the table near by."

Then the *pastor* told of how he had seen spirits in the shape of balls of fire floating through the air. They were souls doing penance for their past sins. As a relief to our fright, Don Francisco suggested that Tío Julianito do one of his original dances to the tune of Alejo's fiddle. A place was cleared on the canvas and that started the evening's merriment.

Border Folklore

T he only occasion when Don Francisco could not be controlled by his wife was when one of his daughters married. Like all fathers of Latin stock, he hated to see his daughters leave the paternal roof. When one married, he would leave the ranch, suicide bound. Armed with a pistol, a knife, a rope, and poison he would escape to the nearest pasture, determined to end his life one way or another. But each time he would return late in the evening after the last guest had departed.

"Francisco, my love, you are an idiot," Doña Margarita would greet him.

"I know it, my pearl," Don Francisco would reply meekly. And with that he would mount his black horse and ride away like lightning to spend his anger on the servants and *peones* who had the misfortune to meet him.

In summer evenings it was customary for San Martín people to gather at the Master's house to shell corn. Don Francisco and his sons were there. Such scenes however, were not for Doña Margarita and her daughter Rosita who sat in the patio of the house. All came: Tío Julianito the shepherd, with his brood of half-naked children over-eager for food, Alejo the fiddler, Miguelito the idiot, called the innocent because the Lord was

This story was published under the general title "Among My People," *Mary Immaculate* XVIII, 7 (1935) 201-206. A different and longer version of this story was published in 1932 in Jovita González "Tales and Songs of the Texas-Mexicans," *Man, Bird and Beast,* ed. J. Frank Dobie (Austin: Folk-Lore Society, 1932) 102-109.

keeping his mind in heaven, Chon the *baciero*. Even the women came for that night Don Francisco was to serve the supper to his people. In the center of a big canvas, spread outside in front of the kitchen were piled pyramids of corn for the shellers who sat in a circle, and shelled the grains off the cob with bare hands.

It was then under the moonlit sky, that the ranch hands and shepherds showed their talent as story tellers, and singers.

"Work is felt less when the mind is occupied with pleasant thoughts," said the master of the house. "Chon will you sing for us?"

The person addressed, a little black-faced, wrinkled old man whose face resembled a bat's solemnly got up, unhooked the lantern from its hook and placed it behind a sack of shelled corn.

This produced a laugh among the spectators. He was so ugly, poor fellow! He did not want anyone to see his facial contortions as he sang. He was a musicless bard who in a sing-song nasal tone chanted short, unintelligible ditties. He sang the romance of the Louse and the Flea, much to the amusement of all.

"*Válgame Dios,*" said Martiniano, one of the cowboys, "what a silly song, but you can't help that, can you, Chon?"

"As fine a song as ever I heard," interceded Don Francisco, "and just to show how pleased I am with it, I am going to tell you a story which my grandfather told me on a night like this. It is a story about the Devil, which he heard from his own grandfather, who got it from a wandering cowboy who might have been Pedro de Urdemañas[†] himself. But before I begin you might cross yourselves and say a prayer, the Evil One may be around and it's always best to be prepared. If you are ready I shall begin:

It was an abnormally hot day in Hell. The big devils and little devils were all busy feeding the fires, making final prepara-

---

[†]Other names for this fictional character of the Spanish oral tradition are: Pedro de Urdemalas, Pedro el de Malas, and Pedro Malasartes, among others.

tions to give a warm reception to a barber, and a banker who had announced their arrival. A timid knock sounded in the door, and Satan, who was sitting on a throne of flames, sent one of his henchmen to see who the arrivals might be. In walked three men. One, razor in hand, gave away his profession; the second held on to a wallet like Judas Iscariot to his; the two were abnormally terrified. The third did not appear a bit impressed by the fiery reception awarded them, but with the coolness and the nonchalance of one accustomed to such things glanced about with a look of curiosity. He was an athletic sort of a man, wore a five-gallon hat, *chivarras* and spurs, and played with a lariat he held in his hands. He seemed to be as much at home as the others were terrified. Before he was assigned any particular work, he walked to where a devil was shoveling coals, and, taking the shovel from his hands, began to work.

Satan was so much impressed that he paid no attention to the others but went to where the stranger was. He did not like this man's attitude at all. He liked to watch the agony on the face of the condemned, but here was this man as cool as a September morn. He went through the flames, over the flames, into the flames and did not mind the heat at all. This was more than his Satanic Majesty could endure. Approaching the man, he commanded him to stop and listen to what he had to say. But the man would not stop and kept on working.

"O, well," said Satan, "if that's the way you feel, keep it up, but I must satisfy your curiosity. I am Pedro de Urdemañas by name. I have lived through the ages deceiving people, living at the expense of women who are foolish enough to fall in love with me. Now as a beggar, now as a blind man I have earned my living. As a gypsy and a horse trader in Spain, then as a soldier of fortune in the new world, I have managed to live without working. I have lived through the equatorial heat of South America, through the cold of the Andes and the desert heat of the Southwest. I am immune to the heat and the cold, and really bask in the warmth of this place."

The Devil was more impressed than ever and wanted to know more of this strange personage.

"Where was your home before you came here?" he continued.

"Oh, in the most wonderful land of all. I am sure you would love it. Have you ever been in Texas?"

The devil shook his head.

"Well, that's where I come from. It is a marvelous country."

"Indeed?" said the Evil One "and what is it like?"

Pedro described the land in such glowing terms that the Devil was getting interested in reality. "And what's more," continued Pedro, "there is plenty of work for you down there."

At this Satan cocked his ears, for if there was one thing he liked better than anything else it was to get more workers for his shops.

"But, listen," he confided, "you say there are many cows there. Well, you see I have never seen one and would not know what to do were I to see one."

"You have nothing to fear about that. There is a marked similarity between you and a cow. Both have horns and a tail. I am sure you and the cows will become very good friends."

"After this comparison, Satan was more anxious than ever to go to this strange land where cows lived.

So early the next day before the Hell-fires were started, he set out earth-bound. Since his most productive work had been done in the cities and he knew nothing of ranch life, Satan left for Texas gaily appareled in the latest city style. He knew how to dress and how he strolled through the earth seeking for Texas, he left many broken hearts in his path.

Finally, on an August day he set foot on a little prairie surrounded by thorny brush, near the lower Rio Grande. It was a hot day indeed. The sand that flew in whirlwinds was hotter than the flames of the infernal region. It burned the Devil's face and scorched his throat. His tongue was swollen; his temples throbbed with the force of a hammer beat. As he staggered panting under the noonday heat, he saw something that gladdened his eyes. A muddy stream glided its way lazily across a sandy bed. His eyes caught sight of a small plant bearing red berries, and his heart gladdened at the sight of it. It was too good to be true. Here was what he most wished for—water and fresh berries to eat. He picked a handful of the ripest and freshest, and with the greediness of the starved put them all into his mouth. With a cry like the bellow of a bull he ducked his head in the stream. He was burning up. The fire that he was used to was nothing compared to the fire from chile peppers that now devoured him.

But he went on, more determined than ever to know all about the land that he had come to see. That afternoon he saw something that, had he not been a devil, would have reminded him of heaven. The ripest of purple figs were growing on a plant that was not a fig tree.

"Here," thought Satan, "is something I can eat without any fear. I remember seeing figs like these in the Garden of Eden." Hungrily he reached for one, but at the first bite he threw it away with a cry of pain. His mouth and tongue were full of thorns. With an oath and a groan he turned from the prickly pear and continued his journey.

Late that same day, just before sunset, he heard the barking of dogs. He continued in the direction from whence the sound came, and soon he came into a ranch house. A group of men, dressed like Pedro de Urdemañas—that new arrival in Hell who had sent him to Texas—ran here and there on horses gesticulating. The sight of them rather cheered Satan up.

And then he saw what Pedro told him he resembled—a cow. Here was a blow indeed. Could he, the king of Hell, look like one of those insipid creatures, devoid of all character and expression? Ah, he would get even with Pedro on his return and send him to the seventh hell, where the greatest sinners were and the fire burnt the hottest. His reflections were interrupted by something that filled him with wonder. One of the mounted men threw a cow down by merely touching his tail. "How marvelous!" thought Satan. "I'll learn the trick so I can have fun with other devils when I go back home."

He approached one of the *vaqueros* and in the suavest of tones said, "My friend, will you tell me what you did to make the lady cow fall?"

The cowboy looked at the city man in surprise, and with a wink at those around him replied, "Sure, just squeeze it's tail."

Satan approached the nearest cow—an old gentle milk cow—gingerly, and squeezed its tail with all his might.

Now, as all of you know, no decent cow will allow any one, even though it be the king of Devils, to take such familiarity with her. She ceased chewing her cud, and, gathering all her strength in her hind legs, shot out a kick that sent Satan whirling through the air.

Very much upset and chagrined, he got up. But what hurt more were the yells of derision that greeted him. Without even looking back, he ran hellbound, and he did not stop until he got home. The first thing he did on his arrival was to expel Pedro de Urdemañas from the infernal region. He would have nothing to do with one who had been the cause of his humiliation. And since then Satan has never been in Texas, and Pedro de Urdemañas still wanders through the Texas ranches always in the shape of some fun-loving *vaquero*.

"That reminds me of something that happened to my father when he was a young man," said Martiniano. "It happened down in the Devil's River, where the Evil One has been locked up in a cave. My father was a God-fearing, truth-loving man, and you can believe his word!"

"One evening as he was sitting on the porch of our house, smoking his after-dinner cigarette, a stranger called on him. He was a handsome man who looked like a Spanish gentleman. He showed a letter of introduction from friends. Being a very hospitable man, my father gave him lodging for as long as he wished to make our home his home.

"He was a cattle buyer. He said he had come to Del Rio to buy stock, and my father introduced him to the ranchmen of the vicinity. There was something strange and mysterious about him, something that made you shrink when you approached him. As long as he stayed in our home he was never known to invoke the name of God or the saints, but as a host it was not my father's duty to question him about his religious convictions.

"One morning as usual, he rode away to the neighboring cattle ranches. At night he did not return. Two days passed and still he did not realize how far ahead of the others he was. So he stopped on the bank of the river to wait. Suddenly, he heard groans coming from the direction of the opposite bank. He swam across and the moans sounded much nearer. Apparently someone was in great pain, for the groans were heart-rending and chilled his blood. He walked along the bank until he came upon a cave formed by the river. The moans were right at his back, and then he realized that someone was in the cave.

"Crouching on all fours, he entered and what he saw was enough to make any stout man tremble. A man buried up to his neck in the sand. His face was gashed and scratched horribly. One of his eyes was black and so swollen that it was closed. His hair was standing on ends. His beard was clotted with blood. The raw nose bone protruded above torn skin. It was the stranger. As soon as he saw my father, he cried out in a piercing voice:

"'Don't come near me. The devil is here. Don't you see him there at the corner of the cave?'

"My father moved nearer.

"'Go back, I tell you. Do you want him to get you as he got me? See how he leers and jeers at me.' And, saying this, the unfortunate stranger tried to bury his head in the sand.

"My father, who had often heard of how the devil had attacked other people, was chilled at horror at what he heard. But he had a Rosary in his pocket and, taking it out, made the sign of the Cross and commanded the evil spirit to depart. He must have left, for the stranger gave a sigh of relief, saying:

"'He has gone. Get me a drink of water.'

"My father left to get the water. When he returned, the Evil Spirit was there again, for the man was shaking and trembling like one possessed and crying out, 'He is there again. Take out your cross.'

"The sign of the cross was made and the man was again at peace.

"He was taken out of the cave and placed on the bank of the river. While my father went to fetch a burro on which to carry him home the man sat by the edge of the river holding the Rosary in his hand.

"Soon the searching party returned and as the man was lifted from the ground to the burro, the Rosary fell from his hands. Something like a whirlwind enveloped the group, and to their consternation both the burro and the rider were carried up in the air. The man screamed, the burro brayed, and the people, realizing the significance of the whole thing said a prayer. A sound like the bellow of a bull was heard up in the air and beast and man fell to the ground.

"For weeks the patient suffered. His physical injuries and the spiritual effects of the devil's visitation had made a wreck of him. When he recovered, a priest was called. The priest heard his confessions and gave him absolution. Then the man told my father what had happened. The morning he left home as he came near

Devil's River he was taken up into the air by what he thought was a whirlwind. However he noticed he was holding on to something slippery, long and slimy. As he looked up he saw the awful face of the devil. He tried to turn loose but the cloven hoofs of the Evil One beat him on the face and his hands were stuck to the tail. Satan took him over the whole town of Del Rio and the cemetery and finally dropped him in the cave. The Evil One then tortured him with his presence and because of that he had buried himself in the sand.

"The stranger stayed until he regained his health and finally disappeared without any explanation. Whether he went home or was carried away by the devil is a thing that has puzzled those who knew him."

"The sweet names of Jesus, Mary and Joseph be our protection."

"And music be our diversion," added Don Francisco realizing the fear of the people gathered there. "Alejo bring your fiddle, María begin the dance." And as Alejo played *Over the Waves* and *Adelita,* fear vanished, and the dancers whirled on the dirt floor and the canvas still covered with grain. The roosters were crowing announcing the coming of another day when the dancers went home. Some to work in the fields, and others to begin their morning chores.

Tales of Mexican Ancestors

The Gift of the Pitahaya

Woman has brought unhappiness to all people, but to the Texas Indians she proved a blessing, for through her the *pitahaya,* a most refreshing fruit, was brought to them.

In east Texas lived a maiden quick as the squirrel, quarrelsome as the magpie, and graceful as a gazelle. As may be imagined, she had more love affairs than a honeycomb had honey. She favored all with a smile but accepted no one. But her father, disgusted with the state of affairs and the great number of warriors who wasted their time courting his daughter, wished to put an end to this shameful situation so little flattering to a chieftain. Calling the maiden to his presence, he commanded her to chose a husband from among the braves gathered there.

"I shall marry only when I please," said the girl haughtily, "but from among them I shall select the warrior who brings me the gift that resembles me most."

The chief no doubt gave a sigh of relief as he saw the suitors leaving. But, soon to the consternation of the father and the merriment of the daughter, they returned. They brought the most unheard of gifts. One who imagined her to be perfect brought a dove, another a milk white fawn. Others brought wild flowers, gay colored feathers and butterflies. And one who imagined his fate as a husband presented a wild cat.

Jovita González, "Tales and Songs of the Texas-Mexicans," *Man, Bird and Beast,* ed. J. Frank Dobie (Austin: Folk-Lore Society, 1932) 101-102.

Although the flowers and butterflies flattered her vanity, the willful princess, who in reality did not want a husband, refused all the gifts. She would have none of these meek braves who wooed her not like warriors should. The suitors did not despair, but the old chief, who saw his tribe in turmoil, did. The cornfields were abandoned, the chase was neglected, and the braves, instead of looking for flints to make arrowheads, scoured the country for presents.

One day heralds announced the coming of a prince from the far away land of the Aztecs. He was tall and straight and walked the village streets in pride and disdain. His look was bold and defiant like the eagle's. The feather mantle he wore rivalled in beauty the flowers of the praire. Heavy bracelets of gold and precious stone circled his arms.

He asked for permission to present his gift to the princess. As the fearless eyes of the maiden met the piercing, dominating look of the warrior, something like lightning flashed through the heavens.

With slow, determined steps he approached her, fixing on her the eyes of a charmer of snakes. He took something from under his mantle and presented it to the princess. It was a *pitahaya* cactus in bloom.

"Princess," he said, "this is symbolic of you who are fair like its flowers, but sharp and forbidding like the thorns that cover it. Under its thorns, however, hides a most delighful fruit, sweet as nectar and refreshing as dew. And you are like that. Under the rudeness and capriciouness hide sweetness and love. That I will discover as I discovered the fruit of the *pitahaya*. Come."

And with his mantle of feathers he covered the maiden, who followed him far south, where the cactus blooms and the mocking bird ever sings of love.

Ambrosio the Indian

If Chon was a heathen, Ambrosio, the Indian cook, was a pagan who never spoke to anyone. And we as children loved to watch him cook and suck the marrow from the bones. He was the barometer of the ranch, for when Ambrosio sang his Indian songs it was a sign of rain. Then the housewives brought in their washings and the children were called indoors, even though not a cloud was in sight.

When he was in a good humor, he was an Aztec; when angry, he claimed to be a wild Apache and then he yelled and whooped in a way that delighted us. But in the spring when the cactus bloomed and the air was fragrant with the prairie flowers, he hummed tunes delightfully soft. It was then that we gathered around him and begged him for a story.

And this is one of them, a myth of remote times when the Indians were lords of the land and the gods walked freely among them. It was told only when the glory of the cactus in bloom brought to the Indian's mind reminiscences of a proud past.

Jovita González, "Tales and Songs of the Texas-Mexicans," *Man, Bird and Beast,* ed. J. Frank Dobie (Austin: Folk-Lore Society, 1932) 98-99.

The First Cactus Blossom

For some unknown crime that had been committed a thing of evil had been sent to punish the Indians. It was a black shapeless beast that walked over the land, flew through the air, burning with his breath all vegetation and living things and blasting all hopes. Sometimes in the shape of an Indian warrior, gloomy and forbidden, he was a forerunner of wars, pestilence and famine. He spoke to no one and no one dared to address him as he passed through the villages, leaving panic behind him. Like all evil things, he was most unhappy and he longed for the conpanionship of man, for the touch of a little child and for the smile of a maiden.

Tired of his solitary life, he went to the medicine men. The solution to his problem was difficult indeed. He would cease to be evil and become a mortal being when a maiden with hair like the rays of the sun, eyes like a royal emerald, and face like a magnolia blossom would allow him to kiss her. And because of this dim hope he grew more restless, tramped over the earth, and brought more death and destruction upon the people.

Now on the hill beyond was the city of the chief who was mighty and brave like the mountain lion. But a strange thing happened in the household of the king. A child was born to him, not bronzed like all people, but fair, with hair like the Sun god's and

Jovita González, "Tales and Songs of the Texas-Mexicans," *Man, Bird and Beast,* ed. J. Frank Dobie (Austin:Folk-Lore Society, 1932) 99-101.

eyes like the emerald. All the soothsayers and witches were called to a council to interpret the meaning of it all.

"Oh, king," said the oldest of all, "a great joy and sorrow awaits thee. This child will bring happiness to your people but only through her death."

Then the king commanded the building of a big house in the heart of a deserted island. A thick cactus wall was built all around it and a double one of maguey. In this island the child and the wisest witch that could be found were placed. In time the cactus grew so tall that the leaves reached the sky and the thorns were so sharp and pointed that not even a bird could fly through the fence.

And the king, seeing that his child was free from harm, was happy.

In the meantime the baby had grown into a lovely maiden. She sang all day and no lover robbed her of her dreams of peace. One night the old witch was awakened by the princess's screams. In her dreams she had been pursued by a black something with huge bat-like wings that filled her with terror. The witch knew that the time appointed by the prophesy was come and she began to study the means of saving her charge. Every night the princess had the same dream and each time the monster came nearer and nearer and scorched her with his fiery breath.

One evening, as the princess was walking by the wall, she was attracted by a waving plume black as night. It reminded her of the dreams she had had, but the voice that called her was sweet like the playing of a reed flute. She approached him and there heard the most wonderful things of the outside world and the people who lived beyond the cactus fence. That night she had the most dreadful dream of all, for the black monster took her in his arms and flew away to unknown regions. The old witch knew then that nothing could now save the princess. She told her good-bye and gave her a cactus thorn, with this admonition, "When in trouble, prick your hand with the thorn and you will be safe."

Next morning the princess heard the song of the unknown warrior. and she came out to meet him. Forgetting himself, forgetting to be gentle, he pressed her into his breast. With a cry of fear she broke loose, for his touch burned like the touch of the black beast of her dreams. She, remembering the cactus thorn, pricked her hand with it as the witch had advised her. To the warrior's antonishment, the princess at once flew into space, getting smaller and smaller, and finally settled on a cactus leaf. But even then she was beautiful, golden and pale. The cactus blossoms have been so ever since.

And then he wept, and, kneeling, kissed the little flower that he had loved so well. As he did so something was born within him—a good heart.

Shades of the Tenth Muses

The air in the room is close and smoky; I can still smell the rosemary and lavender leaves I have just burnt in an incense burned to drive out the mosquitoes that have driven me insane with their monotonous, droning music. For, in spite of the family's efforts to have me work in the house I prefer my garage room with its screenless windows and door, its dizzy floor, the plants of which act like the keys of an old piano, and walls, hung with relics which I like to gather as I go from ranch to ranch in my quest for stories of the ranch folk. A faded Saint Teresa, in a more faded niche smiles her welcome every morning and a Virgin of Guadalupe reminds me daily that I am a descendant of a proud stoic race. Back of the desk, a collection of ranch spits is witness of my ranch heritage, an old, crude treasure chest holds my only possession, a manuscript which will sometime be sold, if I am among the fortunate. Hanging from a nail above is a home-spun, hand-woven coin bag, the very same which my grandfather was given by his mother on his wedding day with the admonition, "my son, may you and all who ever own it keep it filled with gold coins." It hangs there empty, for the descendant of that Don has never seen a gold coin, much less owned one.

In the place of honor, above my desk in a gold and black frame is a prayer, a letter written to the Almighty by my good

---

friend Frost Woodhul, in which he asks for rain, not for himself, but for his friends in the ranches of northern Mexico—"Dear God in Heaven," it begins "Give us rain" . . . and ending "Yours truly."

It is late, too dark to write, the smell of rosemary and lavender is soothing and I fall—can I say asleep? Or am I transported three centuries back?

A figure glides in. It is a woman. She does not see me, or if she does she does not acknowledge my presence. She sits in the vacant chair by my desk. A radiance surrounds her, and I can see her face. She is beautiful, her features patrician and classical in their perfection resemble an ivory cameo, and her eyes are like black diamonds shining in the dark. I am not a bit surprised at the unexpected entrance of my uninvited guest, I even know who she is. She takes paper and pen and begins to write. I don't have to read over her shoulder. I know. She is Sor Juana Inés de la Cruz the spirit of her epoch and her race. I don't know how it happened; I do not even remember having left my place at the desk, yet I find myself resting in the couch. I can not be dreaming; the song of the mocking bird on the telephone past by my window tells me I am awake. And yet another figure equally strange has entered my room. She is a stately matron; her somber dress and serious expression mark her out as one who is always mournful and sad. She sits in the empty chair with a sign and looks around the room. Her eyes become fixed on the prayer. I can see terror and consternation on her face as she reads—"Oh God, our cows are dying; we're not crying. Our tears are dry much like our land. It's rained on every other hand." She clutches at her heart. She gasps at the sacrilegious words. She can not even utter a word.

A clear, silvery laugh bursts from the lips of the nun. "The prayer has shocked you has it not?" she asks.

"You call that prayer? It's blasphemy! Who dares to address God in such familiar terms?"

"I wouldn't say that," answered the nun in a careless drawling tone, "the man no doubt asks for what he wants in his own way. Let me see, who is the author? Frost Woodhul, Judge of Bexar County—not one of us; but I would like to know him. He's witty, I can see and wit, my dear, is a gift from the Angels."

"How can you!" gasps the somber figure. "What did you say his name was?"

"Woodhul, English, perhaps one of your colonials. Do you know him?"

"The Lord deliver me from that! He must be one of the pagan dwellers of Merrill Mount, one of Morton's infidels."

"It's a clever piece of nonsense though," the nun continued, but seeing the look of anguish on her companion's face she said laughing,

"Perhaps he was merely joking."

"Joking about God? That's a sin that would bring fire and brimstone from heaven. Don't you have any religion?"

"Do I have any religion?" laughed the nun, "don't you see these garbs of a servant of the Lord?"

"A nun! And yet you'd like to meet that awful man?"

"My dear, religion and virtue should wear a happy face."

"I don't understand at all. You say you serve the Lord, don't you fear His wrath?"

"I have confidence in His love."

"Who are you? Your words and attitude dismay and yet surprise me."

"Who am I? I am Sister Joan of the Cross. I serve the Lord, and I also write when my duties permit me. People call me the Tenth Muse of New Spain."

"They call you that? What a coincidence! I am also called the Tenth Muse, but of New England."

"Then we should be friends, and know more of each other. Where are you from? Where do you live?"

"I live in Massachusetts, the governor of the colony is my husband, but I was born in England, dear England," Anne Bradstreet, for she is no other, replied sighing again, a tear rolling down her cheeks.

"Why do you weep?"

"For England, for my lovely home, for the friends I left there."

"Don't you like this new place where you live?"

"How can I like it? How can I like the savages, the discomforts of a new country? The ways are so strange! But I am convinced now it is the way of God and to it I must submit. Do you like your country?"

"Do I like it?" answered the nun with shining eyes. "You've never seen anything like the greenness of its valleys, and the blueness of the sky. The air is warm and soft, and the first things my eyes see at dawn are two volcanoes in the distance, covered with perpetual snow! I was born there just twelve leagues from the city of palaces, that's what we call Mexico, and there I would be now had it not been that my thirst for knowledge brought me to the city."

"Oh you like learning too?"

"Yes, I was but three when I learned to read and write, and when I was thirteen my parents presented me to the viceroy who had heard of my learning."

"And when I was seven," answered Anne, "I had as many as eight tutors in languages, dancing and music."

"Strange isn't it that we should like the same things! I love music too; often have I composed selections for the viceroy and his wife, and the Mother Superior."

"Somehow, I can not see you as a nun. You are so gay, so happy, so care free. Why did you enter the convent?"

"In the first place to serve God, and then too I needed a retreat, a quiet place to study, where I might work without interruption, and in the convent I found the things I longed for."

"Aren't you ever lonesome? Don't you crave for the companionship of others?"

"My dear Anne, you don't know much about us, do you?"

"No, I must admit I don't. I have always looked upon nuns and Popish things with distrust, even with fear. Won't you tell me about your life?"

"Delighted. We live in a big, beautiful convent surrounded by luxurious gardens. We never leave it, but we have a life of contentment and leisure. You see all of us there belong to the nobility. We have over two hundred servants who do the work and we lead a life of prayer and innocent pleasures. We are quite experts at making pastries, cakes and sweets, which we send to our friends, in particular to my friend the viceroy. During our leisure hours we embroider altar clothes, converse or play the harp. In the afternoon after vespers we hold open house. The viceroy, the notables and their ladies come. We discuss the events of the day, the gossip of the town, comment on the sermons preached, the last religious festival. There are times though, when the conversation is not so pleasant, and that is when we hear that an English pirate ship has captured a Spanish galleon loaded with gold and silver bars."

"English pirates! We never have been that! Our seamen might capture a Spanish treasure ship but always in a good fight!"

"I do not like to contradict. Pirate or patriot, it is the same. It merely is a matter of point of view. What was I saying? I've lost the trend."

"You discussed the events of the day."

"Oh yes. Our guests sing to us the latest songs, ballads, romances, provincial tunes and they also delight us with the latest dances."

"Dances? Dances? Dear me, dear me, and you a nun! Dancing is an instrument of Satan himself. And I always thought living in the convent was dull."

"Not when you realize our Spanish convents have not been invaded yet by northern prudery and Puritanism. But tell me, how do you employ your time?"

"I am the mother of eight children. I had eight birds hatch in one nest. Four bucks there were, and hens the rest. I nursed them up with pain and care, nor cost, nor labour did I spare. Till at the last they all had wing. And then I have my husband, if ever two were one, then surely we. If ever man were loved by wife then he; if ever wife was happy in a man, compare with me ye women if you can.

"Did you ever want to get married?"

"No, I can not say I ever did. Many suitors wooed and made love to me, but no one would I have. I always thought myself superior to any man."

"You astound me, Juana."

"Why should they be our superiors? Have we not a mind like they? Do we not have a soul? Can we not think? Can we not love the same as they? Are they made of finer clay?"

"Let Greeks be Greeks, and women what they are. Men have precedence and still excel. It is but vain unjustly to wage war: Men can do best, and women know it well."

"I don't know such things! They are weak, silly creatures who can not take the blame for the sins they commit. Foolish, foolish men who blame women for the evil things they do, when they themselves are to blame for the sin women commit! Tell me who is more to blame, although both I think are sinners, the one who hungry sins for pay, or the one who pays to sin?"

"Stop, stop!" Anne called out covering her ears with both hands. "Your evil words pollute me, contaminate me! Have you no decency? No shame?"

"My dear Anne, there is nothing more decent than truth, and there is nothing shameful in seeing life as it is! However, if such things hurt your tender, sensible heart, we shall no more discuss them.

When you came in you told me you were the Tenth Muse; I am curious to know what you've done to merit such title. Have you published any of your poems?"

"I don't like to talk about it. It's too much like vanity, and vanity, as you no doubt know, is a thing of Satan. But if you'll tell me what you've written, perhaps I shall consider . . ."

"I don't mind telling you, I have written three plays and my poems have been published under the title of '*Works of the Only Poetess, Tenth Muse, Sister Juana Inés de la Cruz, Professed Religious in the Monastery of San Gerónimo of the Imperial City of Mexico, which in Various Metres, Languages and Styles, Discusses Many Matters with Elegant, Subtle, Clear, Ingenious, and Useful Verses; for Teaching, Recreation, and Admiration.*' It was published in 1689."

"Your title is as verbose as mine, '*The Tenth Muse Lately Sprung in America. Several Poems, Compiled with Great Variety of Wit and Learning, Full of Delight, Wherein Specially is Contained a Complete Discourse and Description of the Four Elements, Constitutions, Ages of Man, Lessons of the Year. Together with an Exact Epitome of the Four Monarchies, Viz. the Assyrian, Persian, Grecian, Roman, Also a Dialogue Between Old England and New, Concerning the Late Troubles. With Diverse Other Pleasant and Serious Poems.*'"

"As high sounding as mine. What style do you follow?"

"At first I imitated the 'fantastic school' of England, but in spite of that I am told that I made use of ingenious arguments. I would have liked to express my poetic nature, to set forth all that my heart felt, to express my loneliness for England, but I dared not."

"But why, why? Don't you know poets should express their feelings?"

"I dared not, I was touched with maladies of conscience. My Puritan instinct repressed me."

"Pooh, pooh! My dear Anne, you talk like an old woman! I've never been ashamed or afraid to express anything I wish. I discuss earthly love with the same freedom as I do love divine. Love is the spark that keeps us happy."

"Please, Juana, if you talk that way, I shall be forced to leave you. What time is it now?"

The nun looked out the window and without hesitation answered,

"It's eight o'clock by the evening star."

"Dear me, dear me, Simon must be wondering what has become of me. He loves his pipe early, and I must tuck him in bed by mine."

"Simon must be tucked in," giggled the nun to herself, and aloud to Anne she said,

"It has been a great honor and a pleasure to know another Tenth Muse. I thought I had the monopoly to the title. Come up and see me again."

"'Come up and see me.' Where have I heard that before?"

"Never mind, you wouldn't even recognize her name if I told it to you; but do come again."

"That I will my dear Juana," answered the New England Tenth Muse, kissing the nun on the forehead, "but please put that sinful prayer away, I shudder at the levity of it!"

"The one written by your countryman? I really must meet that man; he may not be a poet, but I bet he has a sense of humor and is clever."

Anne faded away. So Juana stood up, yawned, looked at me with what I thought was a wink, and following her companion she also disappeared in the dimness of space.

Tales of Ghosts, Demons, and Buried Treasures

Legends of Ghosts and Treasures

Another class of legends and traditions is equally fascinating, the stories of ghosts and treasure. It is a well known fact that many treasures were buried in Southern Texas and Northern Mexico during the last years of Spanish dominion. Other treasures were hid by the settlers when Indian raids were expected. Stories about such hidden wealth are without number. Wherever a treasure is buried, there is sure to be a ghost or a number of ghosts watching over it. They make their presence known by apparitions, moans, groans, clanking of chains, and clashing of swords.

Nothing so delights the *vaquero* as to sit around a camp fire and tell tales of ghosts, while the flames form weird and fantastic figures and shapes. On one such occasion I heard the story of the Chimeneas Ranch (Chimney Ranch), which is in Maverick County. I shall try to tell it as it was told to me.

It was a cold drizzly afternoon in November. A man in a khaki hunting suit, gun on shoulder, plodded wearly through the gray chaparral. Undoubtedly he was lost, for once in a while he stopped and looked around as if wishing to guide himself by some sign of Nature. A faint cry sounded in the distance. The

---

Jovita González, "Folk-Lore of the Texan-Mexican *Vaquero*," *Texas and Southwestern Lore,* ed. J. Frank Dobie (Austin Folk-Lore Society, 1927) 13-14. A shortened version of this story was republished under the title "The Ghost of Las Chimineas," *Texas Tales,* ed. David K. Sellars (Dallas: Noble and Noble, 1955) 97-106.

hunter stopped, listened attentively, and answered by a loud "Hullo."

Nearer and nearer the cry came. *"Arre, arre, cabras,"* the hunter made out the cry to be. Not far off, half-hidden by *uña de gato* (catsclaw) and mesquites, he distinguished a herd of goats. Then a brown shaggy dog trotted into view. On seeing the hunter, the dog gave a bark, followed by a howl of warning.

"Calla, Lobo, calla," came the cry of the approaching *pastor* (shepherd).

He was a little old man, comical in his ugliness. His wrinkled brown face contrasted with the white of his hair. His toothless grin and his snappy, bright black eyes gave him the appearance of a jack-o'-lantern. The brim of a straw hat jauntily set on his head resembled the halo of a saint. The remains of a Prince Albert coat, gaudily patched, protected him from the rain and cold. Instead of shoes he wore *guaraches* (sandals) of rawhide.

Seeing the hunter, he drew near, "halo" in hand, and, making a bow, said, "Excuse my Lobo, *señor.* He never sees anybody but your most humble servant, and considers everyone else an enemy of the flock. *Calla, Lobo, calla* the *señor* is a friend." The dog probably understood, for he wagged his tail in sign of friendship.

"Can I be of any help to you, *señor?*" the *pastor* added.

"I am lost," the stranger said. "I left camp this morning and got turned around following a wounded deer. I am hungry and cold; a cup of coffee and a fire to dry myself will be all I need. Could you guide me to a ranch house where I can spend the night?"

"The nearest one is some miles off," the *pastor* replied, "but if the *señor* wishes to share the humble home of a poor man, he is most welcome."

The man nodded in silent assent and prepared to follow.

"This way *señor.*"

Night was swiftly descending; and what had been an evening mist was changing to rain. At a turn of the trail they were following, silhouetted against the darkness of the chaparral, was faintly discerned a white mass. As the two approached, the stranger discovered it to be a white stone house semi-hidden by shrubs and *nopal* (prickly pear).

"Didn't you tell me there were no ranch houses near here?" asked the hunter. "What do you call that?"

"Oh, *señor*," replied the *pastor*, "hush! Do not ask me, and *por la Virgen Santa*, do not go in.

"If you want to stay out in the rain, you are perfectly welcome, but as for me I am going in," and forthwith the brusque hunter made a motion towards the house.

"*Señor, señor*, but you'll come to harm."

"But what is wrong with the house?"

"It is a accursed, *señor*," and the *pastor* crossed himself reverently. "The spirits of the dead live there."

"That sounds interesting," the stranger said with a smile of incredulity. "Have your way about it. I will not go in, but you'll have to tell me the story of that house."

"The ghosts do not like the living to speak of them. It molests them, *señor*, and I did not like to do it, but to keep you from harm I will gladly do that and more. Now, *vámonos señor*."

Soon they came to a thached-roofed *jacal* built at the foot of a large mesquite.

"This is your home *a sus órdenes, señor*. Let me build a fire and you will be as comfortable as a king."

As the fire blazed, the stranger said to the goat herder, "I want to hear that story now, *amigo*."

"*Bien*, it is a long story, *señor*. That house we passed was built by an old Spanish family, los Vegas by name, many years ago when Spaniards ruled the land. They built the house well and strong, out of solid rock. In time of danger it was used for a fort, for you can still see the loop-holes on the walls. Some dreadful calamity must have befallen los Vegas, for they disappeared as mysteriously as they came. Some say they were carried away by the Indians; others, that thery were killed by enemies, probably Spaniards. Their blood stains the floors yet. Because there is a fireplace in nearly every room the house has come to be called Las Chimeneas.

"The spirits of los Vegas wander at night. They look for the gold they buried. The American cowboys here call it Mexican superstition, but I swear to you that strange things do happen, *señor*.

"One evening at sundown, as I was returning home with my flock, I heard voices inside of the house. Thinking that some of my friends were there, I stopped. They were talking of something that I did not quite understand, of a duel fought with swords, a murder, a proposed vengance, and of money buried under a certain tree. Then I realized that I had been listening to the voices of the dead. I hurriedly gathered my flock and left.

"Just then José, that worthless fiddler, caught up with me and said meaningly, 'you'll soon be rich, won't you *tío?*'

"No," I answered, "there is not much money in herding goats."

"Dont be so sly, *tío*. What about the legacy of los Vegas?"

"He had also heard, the scoundrel. *Bien, señor*, the next day, taking a pick, I went to the place where I thought the money would be. But I was too late. José had been there before. Queer things happen there, *señor*.

"My wife, Juanita—may her soul rest in peace!—saw an apparition once. She was outside of this very *jacal* watering her flowers. She felt a presence near her; looking up, she saw a beautiful Spanish lady, all dressed in black. She wore a dress like the one *mi señora's* grandmother wore when she was presented to the viceroy in Mexico. She smiled at Juanita. My wife asked her what she wanted, but her reply was a smile; and she faded away. Juanita never forgot that lovely face and smile; she was haunted by it day and night, and like her she faded away. I buried her on the hill top; from here I can see her grave and say an *Ave* for the repose of her soul. Believe me or not, it is the truth.

"That you may believe, I am going to tell you what happened to some American cowboys. They were regular dare-devils, feared neither the dead nor the living. They boosted that they would spend a whole night at Las Chimeneas. Everybody was anxious, of course, to see what the outcome of it would be. They made their preparations in true cowboy fashion. Got their six-shooters in readiness, took enough tobacco to last them a week, and provided themselves with a deck of cards to play poker.

"All went well until midnight. That is the hour when the spirits of the dead wander about. All of the sudden the light went out. Footsteps of someone wearing spurs were heard coming into the room. Of course they said it was the wind—as if the wind could wear spurs. One of them got up, lit the lamp, and the game went on. Again they heard footsteps, and this time they heard the clashing of swords as of combatants fighting a duel. What else happened that night I never knew. Of one thing I am certain. By 4 o'clock that morning the cowboys were camping a mile from the house. Another thing I have noticed is that they do not make fun of me any more, and when I mention Las Chimeneas, they talk of something else or look at each other with a look of alarm.

"It is time to go to bed, *señor*. I hope the ghosts will not molest you. You sleep inside; the rain has stopped; and I will keep watch until the hour of danger has passed. *Hasta mañana, señor*, may the Virgin protect you from all evil spirits."

The War of Independence in Mexico was followed by an exodus of the rich Spanish families who refused to pay allegiance to the newly created empire. Some left by way of Vera Cruz; others came northward towards the frontier. Many reached their destination; others with their wealth were lost, either killed by Indians or dying from exposure. What became of the treasures they carried with them is a question that has occupied the minds of many fortune hunters.

I have heard three stories in regard to these treasures of the exiles. Two are concerning the treasure that is supposedly buried at or near old Las Escobas ranch (*escoba* means *broomweed*), in Starr County.

About the year 1820 a family of wealthy Spaniards came to Ciudad Mier, now in Tamaulipas. They were coming from the interior; the men were well armed and rode pack mules. These were loaded with little chests covered with canvas cloth. They came into the town at nightfall and hurriedly looked for guides that would take them to New Orleans. So great was their hurry that they did not even stop to give the women and children a rest. They crossed the river and came into the province of Texas. But here they met with disaster; their mules would go no farther; two died of fatigue and another broke a leg. After much deliberation, they decided to go on with the women and children and later come back for the gold. The guides were blindfolded and taken to a distant thicket while the treasure was buried in a safe place.

On the return trip, the guides, knowing that they would be immensely rich if they acquired the gold, killed their masters. They came to Las Escobas to look for the buried money, but, search as they might, the exact spot was never found.

Three miles from this ranch is another, Las Víboras (Ranch of the Snakes), where also a treasure was buried. Several years ago, two boys while digging a hole found an ebony tablet buried at the foot of a tree. On it were carved as near as I can remember these ciphers: X..—X..—. As the season in which the tablet was found was very busy, no one paid much attention to it. Later I was told what might be a possible solution.

During the Spanish occupation of Texas a body of soldiers was sent to escort the money that was to pay the garrison at San Antonio. In those days the Comanches were the terror of the border land; they pillaged the ranch houses and murdered the settlers. A band of Indians attacked the soldiers, who unaware, were taking their siesta. A brave resistance was made by the Spaniards, but to no avail, for by evening the last of the guard was killed. Not knowing what to do with money, the Indians buried it somewhere near Las Escobas or Las Víboras.

On what used to be *el camino real,* in what is now Jim Hogg County, is another old Spanish ranch, El Blanco. The place has always been thought to be haunted. Ghosts and spirits in different forms are supposed to haunt a buried treasure. Every *vaquero* when asked about the ghost of El Blanco will give his own version. The following was told me by one named Martiniano.

It was after midnight. Martiniano, the *vaquero*, was returning from a dance. He was happy. No evil thought disturbed his mind, and he whistled to himself as he remembered the pleasures of the *baile.* All of a sudden his horse reared and snorted as if frightened. And a good reason the poor beast had to be so terrified, for there in the middle of the road stood a woman dressed in white, her hair hanging down her back. Giving a sudden leap she grabbed the reins of the horse. Martiniano, as can be imagened, was greatly frightnened, but he had enough presence of mind to ask. "*¿Eres de este mundo o del otro?*" ("Are you from this world or the other?")

"*Del otro*" ("From the other"), the ghost replied. For a while, which seemed an eternity to the *vaquero*, the ghost and the horse struggled. Finally, taking courage, the *vaquero* took out his pistol and shot once, twice, but the ghost held firmer grasp on the reins. About this time the moon came out from behind the cloud, and Martiniano saw the fleshless face of the ghost. As soon as he saw her face to face, the spirit dropped the reins and faded away.

Another *vaquero* told me that on passing by the ranch at night his horse began to limp but he kept going and then, after having traveled all night, at dawn he found himself at the same place from which he had started the night before. Another told me of being attacked by a monster turkey gobbler, and of wrestling all night with it.

The love for music that characterizes all people of Spanish origin is developed to a great extent in the *vaquero*. However, the *vaquero* as a distinct type has not created music of his own. He plays the guitar with mastery, and to its accompaniment sings songs which have been introduced from old Mexico. The theme, as a rule, is of love, of war, of Nature, of the home, and not seldom of animal life. Some of the songs have the vivacious *sal* of the Spaniard, the quick wit of the Andalusian, while others, especially those treating of love, have a certain sadness pelicular to the Mexican peon.

One of the most popular songs that I have heard is *Las Mañanitas de San Juan.* On early, misty spring mornings I have heard the *vaqueros* singing it while saddling their horses.

The Devil on the Border

Si se descuidan
  las jóvenes bellas
El diablo verde
  cargará con ellas.

If the fair maidens
  are not careful
The green devil will
  carry them away.

This is what children are told down at the border when they do not mind their elders about staying indoors during the noon day heat. The Evil One no doubt feels at home during the terrific heat of the noon day hour as he wanders among the ranches of the Rio Grande country. And it is because of this heat no doubt that Satan's visitations to the border country are not uncommon.

I have been told of three such visitations. The first one is a housewife's tale, the place, time and names of the characters being unknown. The second visitation happened recently at a cave near Devil's River in the vicinity of Del Rio and was told to me by a University of Texas student whose father witnessed the incident. The third is an old border legend, very popular because in it the Evil One gets fooled by a *vaquero*.

Jovita González, "Tales and Songs of the Texas-Mexicans," *Man, Bird and Beast,* ed. J. Frank Dobie (Austin: Folk-Lore Society, 1932) 102-109. The story number three of this set of stories about the devil was republished under the title "The Devil in Texas," *A Treasury of Western Folk-lore,* ed. B. A. Botkin (New York: Crown Publishers, 1951) 699-702. The stories number two and three were also published under the general title "Among My People: Border Folklore," *Mary Immaculate* XVIII, 7 (1935) 201-206.

(1)

On an out of the way ranch lived a *vaquero,* poor in the world's goods but blessed with many children. However he did not consider the children a blessing but rather as a curse. When the last one came he was very much vexed and decided to do away with it. The idea of shedding his own baby's blood was repugnant to him. After much thinking he thought of an excellent plan. He placed the child in a box far from the house and sat there day and night to keep his wife from feeding the infant. The baby cried until it got so weak that no sound came from its mouth. All the while the mother, frantic with grief, begged her husband to save the child. But he would not yield. Then, wild in her despair, she cursed him and ended by saying "May the Devil get you."

About midnight of that same day the whole ranch was enveloped in a terrific whirlwind, the smell of sulphur was suffocating, and a dust of ashes choked the people. Above the roaring of the wind a piercing cry of death was heard. No one dared to go to the place where the man and the baby had been, for all remembered the wife's curse.

With the coming of daylight, the people's fears were dispersed and they approached the place. The baby was dead. A white dove, probably its spirit, hovered over the little corpse. As for the man, all that remained of him was a heap of greenish yellow sulphur.

(2)

Now we shall hear in the words of the University student concerning the second apparition as her father saw it.

"The story I am about to tell will not be believed by many, but it really happened down the Devil's River, where the Evil One had been locked up in a cave. It was told to me by my father, a God-fearing, truth-loving man.

"One evening as he was sitting on the porch of our house, smoking his after-dinner cigarette, a stranger called on him. He was a handsome man who looked more like a Spaniard than a Mexican. He showed letters of introduction from friends. Being a very hospitable man, my father gave him lodging for as long as he wished to make our home his home.

"He was a cattle buyer. He said he had come to Del Rio to buy stock, and my father introduced him to the ranchmen of the vicinity. There was something strange and mysterious about him, something that made you shrink when you approached him. As long as he stayed in our house he was never known to invoke the name of God or the saints, but as a host it was not my father's duty to question him about his religious convictions.

"One morning, as usual, he rode away to the neighboring cattle ranches. At night he did not return. Two days passed and still he did not come back. Since every one knew he had several thousand pesos, his disappearance was arousing great curiosity, and since he had been our guest, my father, fearing to arouse suspicion, organized a searching party.

"As he knows every crag, thicket and cave in the Devil's River Country, he led the party. So engrossed was he in his reflections that he did not realize how far ahead of the others he was. So he stopped on the bank of the river to wait. Suddenly he heard groans coming from the direction of the opposite bank. He swam across and the moans sounded much nearer. Apparently someone was in great pain, for the groans were heart-rending and chilled his blood. He walked along the bank until he came upon a cave formed by the river. The moans were right at his back, and then he realized that someone was in the cave.

"Crouching on all fours, he entered and what he saw was enough to make any stout man tremble. A man was buried up to his neck in the sand. His face was gashed and scratched horribly. One of his eyes was black and so swollen that it was closed. His hair was standing on end. His beard was clotted with blood. The raw nose bone protruded above torn skin. It was the stranger. As soon as he saw my father, he cried out in a piercing voice:

"'Don't come near me. The devil is here. Don't you see him there at the corner of the cave?'

"My father moved nearer.

"'Go back, I tell you. Do you want him to get you as he got me? See how he leers and jeers at me.' And saying this, the unfortunate stranger tried to bury his head in the sand.

"My father, who had often heard of how the devil had attacked other people, was chilled with horror at what he heard. But he had a Rosary in his pocket and, taking it out, made the sign of the Cross and commanded the evil spirit to depart. He must have left, for the stranger gave a sigh of relief, saying:

"'He has gone. Get me a drink of water.'

"My father left to go get the water. When he returned, the Evil Spirit was there again, for the man was shaking and trembling like one possessed crying out, 'He is there again. Take out your cross.'

"The sign of the cross was made again and the man was again at peace.

"He was taken out of the cave and placed on the bank of the river. While my father went to fetch a burro on which to carry him home the man sat by the edge of the river holding the Rosary in his hand.

"Soon the searching party returned and as the man was lifted from the ground to the burro, the Rosary fell from his hands. Something like a whirlwind enveloped the group, and to their consternation both the burro and rider were carried up in the air. The man screamed, the burro brayed, and the people, realizing the significance of the whole thing, said a prayer. A sound like the bellow of a bull was heard up in the air and beast and man fell to the ground.

"For weeks the patient suffered. His physical injuries and the psychological effects of the devil's visitation had made a wreck of him. When he recovered, a priest was called. The priest heard his confession and gave him absolution. Then the man told my father what had happened. The morning he left home as he came near Devil's River he was taken up into the air by what he thought was a whirlwind. However he noticed he was holding on to something slippery, long, and slimy. As he looked up he saw the awful face of the devil. He tried to turn loose but the cloven hoofs of the Evil One beat him on the face and his hands were stuck to the tail. Satan took him over the whole town of Del Rio and the cemetery and finally dropped him in the cave. The Evil One then tortured him with his presence and because of that he had buried himself in the sand.

"The stranger stayed until he regained his health and finally disappeared without explanation. Whether he went home or was carried away by the devil is a thing that has puzzled those who knew him."

(3)

It was an abnormally hot day in Hell. The big devils and the small devils were all busy feeding the fires, making final preparations to give a warm reception to a barber, a student, and a banker who had announced their arrival. A timid knock sounded on the door, and Satan, who was sitting on a throne of flames, sent one of his henchmen to see who the arrivals might be. In walked four men. One, razor in hand, gave away his profession; the second held on to a wallet like Judas Iscariot to his; the third exhibited a notebook devoid of notes. The three were abnormally terrified. The fourth did not appear a bit impressed by the fiery reception awarded them, but with the coolness and nonchalance of one accustomed to such things glanced about with look of curiosity. He was an athletic sort of a man, wore a five gallon hat, *chivarras* and spurs, and played with a lariat he held in his hands. He seemed to be as much at home as the others were terrified.

Before he was assigned any particular work, he walked to where a devil was shoveling coals, and, taking the shovel from his hands, began to work. Satan was so much impressed that he paid no attention to the others but went to where the stranger was. He did not like this man's attitude at all. He liked to watch the agony on the face of the condemned, but here was this man as cool as a September morn. He went through the flames, over the flames, into the flames and did not mind the heat at all. This was more than his Satanic Majesty could endure. Approaching the man, he commanded him to stop and listen to what he had to say. But the man would not stop and kept on working.

"O, well," said Satan, "if that's the way you feel keep it up, but I really would like to know something about you and were you come from."

"If that's the case," the stranger replied, "then I feel I must satisfy your curiosity. I am Pedro de Urdemañas by name. I have lived through the ages deceiving people, living at the expense of women who are foolish enough to fall in love with me. Now as a beggar, now as a blind man I have earned my living. As a gypsy and a horse trader in Spain, then as a soldier of fortune in the new world I have managed to live without working. I have lived through the equatorial heat of South America, through the cold of the Andes and the desert heat of the Southwest. I am immune to the heat and the cold, and really bask in the warmth of this place."

The Devil was more impressed than ever and wanted to know more of this strange personage.

"Where was your home before you came here?" he continued

"Oh, in the most wonderful land of all. I am sure you would love it. Have you ever been in Texas?"

The devil shook his head.

"Well, that's where I come from. It is a marvelous country."

"Indeed?" said the Evil One, "and what is it like?"

Pedro described the land in such glowing terms that the Devil was getting interested in reality. "And what's more," continued Pedro, "there is plenty of work for you down there."

At this Satan cocked his ears, for if there was one thing he liked better than anything else it was to get more workers for his shops.

"But, listen," he confided, "you say there are many cows there. Well, you see I have never seen one and would not know what to do were I to see one."

"You have nothing to fear about that. There is a marked similarity between you and a cow. Both have horns and a tail. I am sure you and the cows will become very good friends."

After this comparison, Satan was more anxious than ever to go to this strange land where cows lived.

So early the next day before the Hell fires were started, he set out earth-bound. Since his most productive work had been done in the cities and he knew nothing about ranch life, Satan left for Texas gaily appareled in the latest New York style. He knew how to dress, and as he strolled through the earth seeking for Texas, he left many broken hearts in his path.

Finally, on an August day he set foot on a little prairie surrounded by thorny brush, near the lower Rio Grande. It was a hot day indeed. The sand that flew in whirlwinds was hotter than the flames of the infernal region. It burned the Devil's face and scorched his throat. His tongue was swollen; his temples throbbed with the force of a hammer beat. As he staggered panting under the noonday heat, he saw something that gladdened his eyes. A muddy stream glided its way lazily across a sandy bed. His eyes caught sight of a small plant bearing red berries, and his heart gladdened at the sight of it. It was too good to be true. Here was what he wished for the most—water and fresh berries to eat.

He picked a handful of the ripest and freshest, and with the greediness of the starved put them all into his mouth. With a cry like the bellow of a bull he ducked his head in the stream. He was burning up. The fire that he was used to was nothing compared to the fire from the chile peppers that now devoured him.

But he went on, more determined than ever to know all about the land that he had come to see. That afternoon he saw something that, had he not been a devil, would have reminded him of heaven. The ripest of purple figs were growing on a plant that was not a fig tree.

"Here," though Satan, "is something I can eat without any fear. I remember seeing figs like these in the Garden of Eden." Hungrily he reached for one, but at the first bite he threw it away with a cry of pain. His mouth and tongue were full of thorns. With an oath and a groan he turned from the prickly pear and continued his journey.

Late that same day, just before sunset, he heard the barking of dogs. He continued in the direction from whence the sound came, and soon he came to a ranch house. A group of men, dressed like Pedro de Urdemañas—that new arrival in Hell who had sent him to Texas—ran here and there on horses gesticulating. The sight of them rather cheered Satan up.

And then he saw what Pedro told him he resembled—a cow. Here was a blow indeed. Could he, the king of Hell, look like one of those insipid creatures, devoid of all character and expression? Ah, he would get even with Pedro on his return and send him to the seventh hell, where the greatest sinners were and the fire burned the hottest. His reflections were interrupted by something that filled him with wonder. One of the mounted men threw a cow down by merely touching its tail.[†] "How marvelous!"

[†] The art of throwing a cow by tailing it used to be extensively practiced on Texas ranches. It is known as *colear.*

thought Satan. "I'll learn the trick so I can have fun with the other devils when I go back home."

He approached one of the *vaqueros* and in the suavest of tones said, "My friend, will you tell me what you did to make the lady cow fall?"

The cowboy looked at the city man in surprise, and with a wink at those around him replied, "Sure, just squeeze its tail."

Satan approached the nearest cow—an old gentle milk cow—gingerly, and squeezed its tail with all his might.

Now, as all of you know, no decent cow would allow any one, even though it be the king of Devils, to take such familiarity with her. She ceased chewing her cud, and, gathering all her strength in her hind legs, shot out a kick that sent Satan whirling through the air.

Very much upset and chagrined, he got up. But what hurt more were the yells of derision that greeted him. Without even looking back, he ran hell-bound, and did not stop until he got home. The first thing he did on his arrival was to expel Pedro from the infernal region. He would have nothing to do with one who had been the cause of his humiliation. And since then Satan has never been in Texas, and Pedro de Urdemañas still wanders though the Texas ranches always in the shape of some fun-loving *vaquero*.

Without a Soul

L ate one November afternoon, on All Saints' Day, to be more exact, I went to see my old friend Father José María. I had just discovered an old manuscript and I wanted to consult him concerning its authenticity. The polite, copper-colored maid who came to the door asked me to wait in the living room.

"He is very busy right now," the maid explained, "but I am sure he will see you as soon as he can. Tomorrow is All Souls' Day, the day of the dead, and he has to get ready for the services and the prayers that must be said for the faithful departed."

She left. I lighted a cigarette, and went to the window to watch the always interesting Mexican community. From where I stood I commanded a good view of the street. A cold mist veiled the street in gloom. However, through the thick fog, I noticed directly across from the rectory, an old woman twining white and yellow chrysanthemums into a wreath. "To take to the cemetery

---

The original manuscript of this story is in the *E. E. Mireles & Jovita González de Mireles Papers, Special Collections & Archives, Texas A&M University-Corpus Christi Bell Library. Copyright © Texas A&M University-Corpus Christi. All rights reserved.* Presumably this document is the paper that Jovita González presented at the 1928 Meeting of the Texas Folk-Lore Society entitled "The Woman Who Lost Her Soul." This is a very similar and shortened version of the story that is presented under the general title "Among My People," *The Woman Who Lost Her Soul. A Folklore Story* of the magazine *Mary Immaculate* XVIII, 12 1935: 327-329 and XVIII, 13 1936: 11-12, and to the story that is presented in the Chapter XV "The Woman Who Lost Her Soul" of the novel *Dew on the Thorn* by Jovita González, ed. José Limón (Houston: Arte Público Press, 1997) 157-165. One of the differences between this version of the magazine and the novel with the one that is presented in this collection is that in this one the narrator substitutes herself for Don Francisco and presents the story as a personal field experience.

to her dead," I thought. In the vacant lot beyond, two street vendors offered their wares to the passersby; wilted brown-edged white chrysanthemums, paper flower wreaths and candles.

I heard the six o'clock Angelus ring. I saw the few people on the street stop and bow their head in prayer. Hardly had the last stroke of the bell rung when I heard a shrill cry:

"¡La Desalmada! ¡La Desalmada! The woman without a soul!"

The old woman on the porch dropped her flowers and hastily crossed herself. The two vendors barricaded themselves behind their improvised stalls. As the cry of alarm floated down the street I saw the same signs of fear.

With a natural curiosity I ran out hoping to find out the cause for such sudden alarm. I looked down the street and saw nothing out of the ordinary. I noticed, however, two women, braver than the rest, who standing on the doorsteps of their house, gesticulated wildly and pointed at someone coming down the street.

"Maldita, Accursed," I heard them yell, shaking their fists at a woman in black. The woman stopped as though in fear. She drew a black shawl over her face and in a moment disappeared into the dark alley. Forgetting my mission, forgetting that night was near, I ran after the woman determined to find out more about the strange incident I had just seen.

What had been an evening mist was now turning into a cold rain, but I paid no attention. She turned from one crooked alley into another. I followed fascinated by a morbid curiosity. At the end of a blind alley I saw her enter a hut; hurriedly closing the door behind her. I pushed. The door was locked. I knocked; no answer. I knocked again and again. A trembling voice, like that of a frightened child, asked:

"What do you want?"

"I want to see you; let me in."

"But you cannot come near me, Señor, I am accursed, I am La Desalmada."

"*¿La Desalmada?*"

"Yes, the woman without a soul."

"I know that," I replied, humoring her, not having the least idea what she meant.

"Do you really want to see me?"

"Yes, yes, open the door."

"Let me unlock it then."

I entered. The room, if it could be called that, was dark and damp. A sputtering, tallow candle furnished the only light. By it I could see that the woman before me was beautiful, but beautiful in an unearthly way. Her face, pale as wax, reminded me of an ivory medieval statue. Her eyes were black, fathomless pools, shimmering like black diamonds in the night.

"You" I stammered, not knowing how to begin.

"Yes, *Señor,* I have no soul," she said with the simplicity and conviction of a child. "You are not afraid to be with me?" she asked. "You are the only one that has come near me in such a long time—and for that I am very grateful. Because you have been kind to me, and that others may profit by my sinful action, I will tell you my story. But you must promise to tell it again and again. Do you swear it by the ashes of your ancestors? Do you swear by the salvation of your soul?"

I nodded my head in silent assent.

"May your children, and your children's children be stung by scorpions and devoured by worms, if you fail to keep your promise. But please sit down. I am sorry I have no better seat to offer you," she said as she pointed to an empty apple box.

Like one in a trance I sat down, my eyes fixed on hers.

"I have not always been as you see me now," she began, "Once I had a home and was happy; and because my parents had no other children I was spoiled and selfish. Our friends considered me beautiful and were proud of me. No one could play the guitar and sing as I could; and when I danced, the castanets fluttered like black butterflies in my hands. The praises of those who knew me turned my head and I became arrogant and haughty. My admirers were many. In the mellow evenings of summer, when the perfume of the night blossoms, and the singing of the birds intoxicated the senses of youth with the gladness of living, I was serenaded by someone who courted my love. It was not uncommon to hear a serenader, in the early morning hours, singing a love song at my window.

"Like all the girls of my class I lived a life of seclusion; was not permitted the company of young men. But what does that matter when flashing dark eyes speak? I encouraged all, but I accepted no one. Why did I not marry? Because my perverse nature wanted the only thing that I could not have. I loved Julio, the promised husband of Rosario, my best friend. My eyes told him what my lips could not say. Every evening, when all was quiet, he came to the *reja* of the window to talk to me. At this time something happened that made me more determined than ever to keep Julio for myself. The month of May came around, and with it the coronation of Our Blessed Mother, and when Rosario was chosen to crown the Virgin, my heart was filled with anger and envy. Why should she who was plain have everything while I who was beautiful had nothing?

"As the day of the ceremony drew near, Julio's love making became more ardent and persistent. I promised to give him my answer after the Virgin's coronation. That evening always will live in my mind. The Virgin herself must have blessed it. Balmy, yet cool, sweet-scented with many flowers. The white-clad, white veiled girls, the singing of the *Ave María,* and the flickering of the candles in the dusk, as we wended our way into the church, made me forget all but that I was a child of Mary. As I knelt at the Virgin's feet to offer my flowers, I also left another offering, my love for Julio—I gave it up that Rosario might be happy.

"When he came to see me I told him of my resolution. I let him see the enormity of our sin and our wickedness! I urged him not to see me again. How bitter our parting was! But in spite of the heartache, I felt free and light-hearted because of my sacrifice. As Julio kissed my hand for the last time, Rosario came into the room. She did not say anything. Neither did I. I had no explanation to offer. 'She will know all from him when he sees her later this evening,' I thought, for he had promised me to call on her that night.

"Early next morning as I was watering the flowers in the patio, Rosario came in, pale as death. She gasped a few words and fell at my feet. She was dead. She held something white in her hand. It was a note addressed to me. 'You have tortured me on earth,' it said, 'my spirit will torture yours in Hell.'

"No sooner was Rosario dead than my soul began to be tormented. Call it remorse, call it Hell, or what you may, my soul was in agony. My parents, disgraced because of the shame that had come to them because of my bad behavior, disowned me; my old friends shunned me as one unclean. My mother took to her bed, and when she was buried a few days later, my father and I were the only ones who accompanied her to her resting-place. My father left town but I could not. Something, some unknown force kept me close to the grave of my victim.

"Now I am as one unclean, a living corpse, for my soul is with my victim in Hell. I can not eat; I can not sleep. I tramp the streets in hopes that the weariness of my body will make me forget. At this time of the year, as the day of the dead gets near, Rosario comes to haunt me in my dreams. First as an indistinct shadow which gradually takes shape. Then I see her as I saw her last. Her eyes pierce me like a dagger and with a cry of anguish her voice rings out, 'My spirit suffers in Hell because of you.' I wake up in despair—Oh! The agony, the sufferings and remorse of a lost soul!

"I have been to see the priest that christened me and prepared me for my first Communion. I opened my heart to him as I have to you now. There were tears in his eyes as he listened to my story."

"'My child, my child,' he said, 'you have no doubt sinned, but your soul is where it should be, in God's keeping. Pray much, eat well, and end your life of wandering.'

"I followed his advice and for a time felt better and had hopes of being happy again. But one night, I saw Rosario again. She was surrounded by flames and writhing in agony. The torments she suffered drove me insane.

"In desperation I went to see a gypsy witch, a fortune teller. What she told me filled me with terror. My soul, she said, was in the liver of a toad. Only through many incantations would it be restored to its proper place.

As she said the last words her eyes became distorted with fear. Like one in pain she shrieked, her trembling hand pointing to a dark corner of the room.

"It comes—it comes—for my soul!"

A toad hopped into the middle of the room blinking its eyes solemnly. The woman fell on the floor, moaning:

"My soul is gone—my soul is lost!"

The Woman Who Lost Her Soul

L ate in the afternoon Don Francisco was sitting in the Rectory waiting for his old friend Father José María. A polite cop-
per-hued maid had told him that the priest would see him in an
hour; and having nothing with which to occupy himself he stood
at one of the windows to view the town and watch the passersby.
From the courtyard opposite the parish school came the sound of
children's voices, now urging some one to make a home run, now
cheering the victor, now showering strong Spanish interjections
with Latin vehemence on the defeated. Outside the glorious sun-
shine of a Texas afternoon. The last rays of the sun tinted the blue
sky with brilliant hues, garnet, purple, and gold; a gay colored
sky, a gay colored neighborhood. Here, an adobe house painted
a brilliant blue, there a tin roofed shack shamelessly flaunted its
title to the world, *El Viento Libre* (Free Air). In the house beyond,
sitting on a vine-clad porch, a black-haired girl lazily strummed
the guitar. Across the street two youths plucked feathers from
their game cocks to arouse their fighting spirit for the next day's
fight. The langorous indolence pervading the atmosphere was

Jovita González published this story in the XVIII, 12 1935: 327-329 and XVIII, 13 1936: 11-12
issues of *Mary Immaculate* magazine, under the general title "Among My People." Jovita
González presented this story in a more abbreviated version at the 1928 meeting of the Texas
Folk-Lore Society. By carefully integrating the various versions of this story, José E. Limón
achieved its edition in: Jovita González, *Dew on the Thorn,* ed. José E. Limón (Houston: Arte
Público Press, 1997) 157-165. The version of the story published in this collection belongs to the
one presented in the *Mary Immaculate* magazine.

that easy going way peculiar to the Mexican temperament. This quietude and stillness was broken by a childish cry:

"*La Desalmada, La Desalmada.*"

The girl on the porch presumably frightened, dropped her guitar and hastily crossed herself. The children in the school yard ceased their play; even the youths ran into the yard roosters under arms. As the cry of alarm floated down the narrow street the same demonstrations of fear were shown. With a natural curiosity Don Francisco looked down the street to find out the reason for such demonstrations of fear. He peered down the street and saw nothing alarming. He noticed, however, two women braver than the rest, standing on the door steps, gesticulating and uttering curses on some one coming down the street.

"*Maldita, Maldita,*" (accursed, accursed) they yelled threateningly, shaking their fists at a woman in black. She stopped as though in fear, drew her black shawl over her face, and in a moment disappeared into a dark alley. Forgetting his mission, forgetting that it would soon be night, Don Francisco ran out of the room determined to find out more of this strange personage.

Stumbling over the rocks and rugged cracks, he followed the fleeting black figure which, like a soul in pain, glided into the darkness. The chase continued. She turned from one dark alley into another. He followed fascinated by a morbid curiosity. At the end of a blind alley she entered a hut and hurriedly closed the door behind her. He pushed; the door was locked. He knocked; no answer. Don Francisco knocked again and again. A voice trembling like that of a frightened child asked:

"What do you want?"

"Let me in," he replied, "I must see you."

"But you cannot, *señor*, I am accursed, I am *La Desalmada.*"

"*¿La Desalmada?*"

"Yes, the woman without a soul."

"I must see you then, I am looking for you," he replied, humoring her, not having the least idea what she meant.

"Just a moment then, let me unlock the door."

He entered. The room, if it could be called that, was dark and damp. A sputtering tallow candle furnished the only light. By it he could see that the woman before him was beautiful, but beautiful in an unearthly way. Her oval face, pale as wax, reminded him of an ivory statue. And her eyes were dark fathomless pools, shimmering like black diamonds in the night.

"You," he stammered, not knowing how to continue.

"Yes, *señor*, I have no soul," she said with the simplicity and conviction of a child.

"If you really want to know, *señor*, I will tell you my story; but you must swear never to repeat it, never to repeat what I am going to say to you. Do you swear by the ahses of your ancestors? Do you swear by the salvation of your soul?"

He assented.

"May your children and your children's children be stung by scorpions and devoured by worms if you ever betray my secret. But please sit down *señor*, and I will tell you all.

"I have not always been as you see me now. Once I had a home and was happy, and because my parents had no other children I was spoiled and very selfish. Our friends considered me beautiful and were proud of my accomplishments. No one could play the guitar and sing as I could, and the castanets as they clicked merrily in the mad whirl of the dance fluttered like black butterflies amidst the hail. The praises of those who knew me turned my head and I became arrogant and haughty. My admirers were many, and in the warm mellow evenings of summer when the perfume of the jasmins in blossom and the singing of the birds in the *huisaches* intoxicated the senses of youth with the gladness of living, I was serenaded by someone who courted my love. It was not uncommon to hear a serenader in the early morning hours when all was covered with dew, singing a love song at my window."

"Like all the Mexican girls of my class I lived a life of seclusion, was not permitted the company of young men. But what does that matter when flashing dark eyes speak? Although I encouraged all, I accepted no one. Why did I not marry? Because my perverse nature wanted the only thing that I could not have. I loved the only man whose love was prohibited by all that was true. I loved Julio, the promised husband of Rosario, my best friend. My eyes told him what my lips would not utter and every evening when all was quiet he came to the *reja* to talk to me. At this time something happened that made me more determined than ever to keep Julio for myself. The month of May came around, and with it the coronation of our Blessed Mother, and when Rosario was chosen to crown the Virgin, my heart was filled with anger and envy. Why should she have everything while I had nothing?

"As the day of the ceremony approached, Julio's love making became more ardent and persistent, and I promised to give him my answer that night. That day will always live in my mind. The Virgin herself must have blessed it. It was bright and yet cool, and the flowers had never been so dewy and so fragrant. The white-clad, white veiled girls, the singing of the *Ave María*, and the flickering of the candles in the dusk as we wended our way into the church made me forget all but that I was a child of Mary. And as I knelt at her feet, I not only gave her my flowers but I gave up my love for Julio.

"He came to see me that night and I told him of my resolution. I let him see the enormity of our sin and our wickedness, and I urged him not to see me again. How bitter our parting was. In spite of the heartache I felt light-hearted because our sacrifice would make Rosario happy. As Julio kissed my hand in a last farewell Rosario came in. She was not the kind that would say much and since I was sick with remorse I did not offer any explanation. 'She will know all from him when he sees her later in the evening,' I thought, for he had promised to call on her that night.

"Early next morning as I was watering the flowers in the patio, Rosario came in pale as death. She gasped a few words and fell at my feet. She was dead. She held something white in her hand. It was a note addressed to me. 'You have tortured me on earth,' it said, 'my spirit will torture yours from Hell.'

"No sooner was Rosario dead than my soul began to be tormented. Call it remorse, call it Hell, or what you may, my soul was in agony. My parents, disgraced because of the shame that had fallen upon them through my bad behavior disowned me, and I was shunned by our former friends as one unclean. My mother took to her bed and when she was buried a few days later my father and I were the only ones who accompanied her to her resting place. My father left town but I could not. Something, some unknown force kept me close to the grave of my victim.

"Now I am as one unclean, a living corpse, for my soul is with my victim in Hell. I cannot eat, I cannot sleep; I tramp the streets in hopes that the weariness of my body will make me forget. Sometimes at night when tired of the day's wanderings I close my eyes in sleep, Rosario comes to haunt me, an indistinct shadow that gradually takes shape. Then I see her as I saw her last. Her eyes piercing me like a dagger and with a cry of anguish her voice rings out, 'My spirit suffers in Hell because of you!' I wake up in despair—Oh, the agony, the suffering and remorse of a lost soul.

"Once I went to see Father José María, the priest that christened me and prepared me for my first Communion. I opened my heart to him. There were tears in his eyes as he listened to my story.

"'My child, my child,' he said, 'you have no doubt sinned, but your soul is where it should be, in God's keeping. Pray much, eat well, work, and end your life of wandering.'

"I followed his advice and for a time felt better and had hopes of being happy again. But one night I saw Rosario again, surrounded by flames and writhing in agony. The torments she suffered drove me insane.

"In desperation I went to see a gypsy witch and fortune teller and what she told me filled me with terror. My soul, she said was in the liver of a toad, and only through many incantations would it be restored to its proper place."

As she said this her eyes became distorted with fear. Like one in pain she shrieked, her trembling hand pointing to a dark corner of the room.

"It comes—it comes—for my soul."

A toad hopped into the middle of the room blinking its eyes solemnly. The woman lay moaning on the floor.

"My soul is gone—my soul is lost."

Don Francisco had heard many supernatural stories in his life, but none so fantastic as what he had just heard. The woman now in convulsions, screamed spasmodically foaming at the mouth and clutching at her heart. Little by little she became more calm, only to remain in a heavy stupor. He looked around for a bed where she might be carried to; but the only thing resembling one was a pallet on the floor. He did all that he could for her, laying her on the bed and wiping the perspiration off her face with a wet cloth.

It was night when he left the hut, but before going back to his wife and daughter he must see the priest and explain his sudden departure. He directed his footsteps to the Rectory where Father José María was wondering what became of him.

"What could have happened," muttered the priest to himself, as he took his after-supper walk in the garden. "It is not like Francisco to run off without seeing me first. I must call on Margarita tomorrow. I wonder if the rumors I have heard about Carlos have reached him? What a terrible situation that is; Don Ramón's stubbornness, Francisco's squeamishness about what he calls family honor, Carlos' compromising silence, and Rosita's broken heart. She is the one who suffers most, but like the angel of God that she is, she smiles and is patient though it is breaking her heart.

～ ～ ～

Don Francisco's footsteps interrupted the priest's thoughts. "You must pardon my abrupt departure," explained the ranchman after the usual salutation, but when I tell you my strange adventure and the strange story I have just heard, you will surely forgive me."

"That's poor Carmen," answered the priest when Don Francisco had finished the story. "She was and still is a good girl. The trouble is that she took the affair too much to heart. She was somewhat to blame, it is true, but not altogether. I have often talked to her, but my words mean nothing. What happened was a terrible thing, of course, that cannot be denied. But I blame her parents more than I do her. They spoiled the girl, encouraged her vain ways, were proud of her conquests, thought her coquettish ways charming, and then when she needed their help most they disowned her, and left her to bear the scandal and gossip alone. I cannot understand a parent's love that cannot forgive the misfortune that comes to a son or daughter. They call it disgrace, shame, dishonor, and instead of kissing the sorrow away, instead of clasping the wayward child to their breast, they cast him away, perhaps to lose his life and what is more precious, his soul. Take Carlos for example—"

"Father, as much as I respect you I must beg you not to speak of him."

"How do you know he is guilty?" the priest interrupted. "His father did a monstrous thing."

"He who is with wolves learns to howl, Father, says the proverb what was he doing in such company?"

"Was he ever given a chance to explain himself? Did Don Ramón for one moment give him the benefit of the doubt? He took it for granted that the boy was guilty; and then, in the presence of all whipped him as though he had been a criminal; shaming him before all, breaking his pride and his spirit. No, no, Francisco, you may think the same as Don Ramón, but let me tell you this: his father and all who countenanced the affair did him a terrible injustice."

"You are a priest, Father, and cannot see the ways of the world."

"The ways of the world, humph," responded the priest scornfully, "I suppose you think they are superior to the laws of God?"

"But honor—"

"Honor is all you can think about. You'd sacrifice your flesh and blood for that. But let me tell you this, and you tell that stone-headed friend of yours the same thing. I am for the boy and until convinced of his guilt, I shall stand for him. And what's more I am going to investigate the matter; not for his Father's sake, not for Rita's, poor unbalanced creature that she is, but for Rosita's."

"As a father I must ask you not to interfere with the paternal discipline."

"And, I as her spiritual father will do everything to bring about her happiness. Don't misunderstand me, Francisco, never will I council her to dishonor you, never will I advise her to go contrary to your wishes, but as one interested in her happiness I will fight for her. Have you heard what people are saying about Carlos?"

"I have not, and I do not wish to hear it."

"Francisco," said the priest placing his hand on his friend's shoulder, "I have always considered you a man of sense, a lover of justice, and I do not want to have to change my opinion of you."

"Well speak then, I shall hear."

"He has left Camargo for Durango, to work in the silver mines. Before leaving he told friends he was going away to get rich, but that he would return to clear his name and marry your daughter."

"How dare he," sputtered the ranchman losing his composure again.

"A man in love dares all. 'I shall return to proclaim my innocence,' he said and I believe in him. But going back to poor Carmen—"

"I came here with the best intentions in the world of doing something for her, but your words have completely upset me and I do not know, Father—I cannot think right."

"Come, come, if your intentions were of that kind, you certainly can change them."

"I had thought that perhaps taking her to the San Martín Ranch might help her—but now I do not know."

"Now you shall do it, my son," said the priest embracing him. "You would be the best of men were it not for your stubborness. That will be heaven for the poor girl; not to be here where every one knows her, not to have to face the scorn of those whom she once loved."

"Don't count on it too much, Margarita might not consent, I have not talked to her yet."

"Of course she will not object, just wait and see."

"We shall talk about this tomorrow. I really must go now, Margarita will be wondering what has become of me. Until tomorrow, Father, come to see us, we are at Don Adán's as usual."

The following morning Don Francisco accompanied by his wife and Father José María went to see Carmen. They found her oblivious to everything, sprinkling the damp dirt floor of the *jacal.*

"That's all she does," whispered the priest to his companion, "believing that her soul is in a toad, she keeps the place damp and cool that it may not go away."

"*Pobrecita,* how terrible that must be," exclaimed Doña Margarita, wiping the tears from her eyes.

"*Buenos días* Carmen." Father José María hoped to bring her out from her trance-like condition with a loud threatening voice. She dropped the bucket, stared at her visitors and then with the steps of a sonambulist walked towards the priest. With trembling fingers she touched his cassock, ran her hands down his sleeve, and at the touch of the Crucifix at his belt, withdrew her hand quickly. She looked at his face again, then at the Crucifix, and finally a smile of recognition shone on her face.

"Father,—Father José María," she stammered.

"Yes, Carmen, we have come to take you away."

"Take—me—away?"

"Yes, my child, to a beautiful place, away in the country, where there are many trees and flowers and where there will be someone to love and care for you."

"Love—me—. Care for me. Oh, Father," she sobbed, "That cannot be. I have not heard those words since Rosario died." ˆ

"Go to her, Margarita," commanded Don Francisco.

"We love you, Carmen, and we want you to come with us, won't you, dear?" said Doña Margarita holding the girl close to her heart.

"But my soul—it is here—I cannot go."

"Of course you can, Carmen, we shall make you well again."

"My soul, Father," she said turning to the priest, "can I go and leave it here?"

"Your soul, dear child, is within you and God will look after it."

"It is in the toad, the gypsy woman told me so," she added with the conviction of a child.

"Carmen," said the priest sternly, putting his hands on her shoulders. "Listen to me, listen closely. You believe me; don't you?" The girl nodded. "Fine. Now listen closely, very closely, to what I am going to tell you. I, Father José María, say this to you. Your soul is safe. It is in God's keeping. You understand?"

"You mean that I am free?"

"Yes, free to go with us who are your friends."

"And can I go now?"

"Yes, dear Carmen, come with us now," and saying this Doña Margarita led the girl by the arm out of the miserable hovel.

"Perhaps with love and care she can become her old self again. Who knows what this will do for her. You are a good man, Francisco. Write me soon and tell me how she gets along."

"Father, there is something I must tell you; it has been on my mind since I talked to you last night. Ramón might have been wrong."

"God bless you, Francisco," and the good priest wrung his hand. He said no more, knowing how much that confession had cost Don Francisco.

The family coach, driven by four white mules, drove into the ranch late that evening. With a leap, Don Francisco descended from the driver's seat, helped the three women down, led them to the door of the *sala* and excused himself. He went into the kitchen where Marcos the outrider had preceded him.

"She looks like a ghost and is crazy," he heard Marcos say. Those were the last words the peon said. The lash of a whip cut him across the face. Don Francisco, eyebrows contracted in a frown, one higher than the other, stood whip in hand facing the men gathering there.

"Let that be a lesson to your lying tongue," he said, "she is not crazy. And whoever repeats that will live to rue the day."

Nana Chita

L ast summer I attended a family gathering to celebrate the return of "our boys" from overseas. By "our boys," we meant the cousins who had grown up together at the old family ranch in Starr County. All were there except Ernesto, the youngest of us all, who had died in the African campaign.

After dinner, as was customary, we sat in the patio to drink our coffee. We reminisced about many childhood incidents and then the topic turned to Nana Chita.

"Her memory made Ernesto have a happy death," José René, just returned from Europe remarked. "We were together when he fell. When I picked him up, both of us knew the end had come. I carried him to shelter behind a ruined wall. I wanted to pray for him and with him—but I could not remember a single prayer. Kneeling by his side, I eased his head on my breast, 'I am not afraid', he whispered, 'Nana Chita . . . the Good Souls . . . remember?' He smiled and was gone.

"Those were his last words. He had gone to Nana Chita and the Good Souls she talked so much about."

No one said much after that; but I am sure we were all thinking of the old woman who had spanked and scolded four generations of our family and had entertained us with her stories.

Nana Chita had been Grandfather's nurse. Past ninety, I remember her as a small, agile old woman, sprite in walk, and tart in talk. Her quick movements and chirpy voice reminded us of a little brown wren. She was a favorite of the twenty-two grandchildren, who at one time or another swarmed the ranch house. We loved her for she was a wonderful person indeed. Her accomplishments were many; she was a marvelous story teller, had "symptom" about supernatural things and she made the most wonderful flour tortillas.

Oh, those tasty, brown, crisp tortillas, baked on the griddle over the coals of the open fireplace! What if Nana Chita did not use the most sanitary methods in her cooking? Our mothers would, no doubt, have kept us away from her kitchen had they known how these crunchy delicacies were cooked.

How fascinating it was to see the round flat cakes, puff up, but more fascinating still was to see her break the air bubbles with a black horn hairpin she used for the three-fold purpose of pinning her hair, picking her tooth and pricking the air bubbles on the tortillas.

"People are like that," she philosophized, sticking the hairpin viciously into the bubble—"they get big and puffed up about nothing—but of course, you can't prick them like you can a tortilla." We, who love her so much agreed, of course, to that. Another source of attraction was the fact that she always kept dry venison hanging from a smoky beam in the kitchen. After the tortillas were baked, she threw a piece of *jerky* into the coals. Our mouths watered as we saw the meat curl around the edges, then get brown and crisp. How wonderful it was to inhale the fragrant, pungent aroma as it cooked! Eyes popping with excitement, we watched her jerk the meat out of the fire, with fingers now immune to the heat from constant handling of the live coals. With sizzling fat still dripping from it, she cut the meat into small pieces, wrapped one of her tortillas around it and with a chirp and a toothless grin, handed it to each of us. That was the official dismissal for the day.

On winter nights, when the grown ups entertained a neighboring ranch family we were sent to *el corredor.* This was a long, closed in porch in back of the kitchen. Its shiny, red brick floor, raised open fireplace, and cots along the wall made it a favorite place for us. We were turned over to Nana Chita, who kept us subdued with stories of the supernatural.

Her stories of lost, wandering souls, made delightful, cold creeps run up and down our spine. The more timid of us snuggled close to her, often hiding our face under the black, woolen, shawl she wore, fearful of seeing a poor lost soul bowed by the weight of its sins.

"There are good souls; and there are bad souls, and they wander through space doing good and doing ill to people," she would begin. "I believe they exist as sure as I know I am sitting here, talking to you. They are everywhere. If they are good souls they like pleasant places, the cenizo in bloom, a flower scented prairie. Have you children ever heard the rustling sound that comes from a cornfield? Sometimes it is soft, like the sigh of a sleeping child. Again it sounds like the echo of distant voices. That's the voice of the Good Souls talking to each other. At times they prefer a room where a baby sleeps. When a baby smiles in his sleep he is at play with them."

"But the bad ones, Nana—Where are they? Do they come near us?" one of us would ask shudderingly.

"The evil ones," Nana Chita explained in an awed voice, "haunt the dark, silent places. They hate the light and run away from all good people. That is, unless they want to harm them. I have seen them, like balls of fire, arising from bone yards and cemeteries; as big bat-like birds which have no place to go, and again as toads that hop about in damp, cold places."

"Please, Nana," begged Ernesto one night, "tell us a story about a Good Soul."

"Of course, my little Mouse," she answered stroking his hair. "Get close so I won't have to speak so loud. The Good Souls don't like for people to get too familiar with them."

Clearing her voice, she began:

"My grandmother, may her soul rest in peace, was your grandmother's maid and lived in this very house with the master's family. As a girl she was very fond of flowers and birds. When she was not weeding the rose garden or watering the pot plants, she was taming baby mocking birds and baby cardinals for her mistress' cages that hung from the arches of the patio.

"One morning, having gotten up late (she had gone to a dance the night before) much to her surprise, she found the rose bed watered and the birds fed. She knew the other servants had not done it because that was her special work. She asked her father if he had done it, but he knew nothing about it. Perhaps Felipe was responsible for the good deed, she thought blushingly. She married him later, you know. But when he was asked, he stammered a denial. She gave it no more thought. The following morning, however, not only had the birds been fed and the garden watered, but the patio was well swept and sprinkled. She inquired among all her neighbors, but she got no satisfaction. As this happened again and again, her father and mother became alarmed. As to my grandmother, she knew she was under a spell and began to lose weight and sleep. An old woman, who knew everything about the things of this world and of the other as well, was consulted.

"'Some spirit in need of prayers is doing your work,' she said. 'Wait until the moon is on the wane, and get up at midnight. Go to the garden and wait. Do not be afraid of anything or anyone. When you see someone coming into the garden say these words,

> *Come out, come forth, come out,*
> *Soul that suffers pains,*
> *A Rosary will I repeat*
> *To break away your chains.'*

"She did as she was told. She went to the window, just as the moon, a mere crescent was coming up. By the dim light she saw a black figure, small and stooped shouldered, busily sweeping. Making the sign of the cross, she called out,

'In the name of the Holy Souls of Purgatory, I command you to tell me who you are and what you want.'

"Hearing this, the figure stopped for a brief moment, looked her in the face for a second and continued her sweeping.

"'Stop your work! I command you in the name of God!' she called again. The old woman stopped. She was a frail, little woman and her face was so lined and so weary, it made you want to cry. Again my grandmother asked her the same question.

"'I was your mother's closest friend,' she answered, 'and have been dead these many years. Just before my marriage I gave her some wool to card and because I was vain and wanted a foolish piece of red ribbon, I used the money which would have paid her. I tried again and again to pay the debt, but my family was increasing so much, and needed so many things, I could never get the money together. My soul can find no rest until the debt is paid. I have plowed fields, ground corn on the *metate.* I have carried water from the well for many members of your family, but no one until now had ever noticed me. I am so tired and in so much need of rest.'

"'What can I do for you?' Grandmother asked very much frightened. 'Forgive my debt, that I may rest.'"

She made the good sign and the old woman faded away.

"Now go to bed, all of you. The Good Souls will take care of you while you sleep."

We never doubted her words. To us her words were like the Gospel. That's why Ernesto had not been afraid to go. He knew Nana Chita and the Good Souls would take care of him.